ECO WARRIOR

WITHDRAWN FROM COLLECTION
VPL
D1459648

OTHER BOOKS BY
PHILIP ROY

Jellybean Mouse (2014)

Mouse Tales (2014)

Me & Mr. Bell (2013)

Seas of South Africa (2013)

Frères de sang à Louisbourg (2013)

Blood Brothers in Louisbourg (2012)

Outlaw in India (2012)

Ghosts of the Pacific (2011)

River Odyssey (2010)

Journey to Atlantis (2009)

Submarine Outlaw (2008)

Eco
Warrior

Philip Roy

RONSDALE PRESS

ECO WARRIOR
Copyright © 2015 Philip Roy

All rights reserved. No part of this publication may be reproduced, stored in a retrieval system, or transmitted, in any form or by any means, without prior written permission of the publisher, or, in Canada, in the case of photocopying or other reprographic copying, a licence from Access Copyright (the Canadian Copyright Licensing Agency).

RONSDALE PRESS
3350 West 21st Avenue, Vancouver, B.C., Canada V6S 1G7
www.ronsdalepress.com

Typesetting: Julie Cochrane, in Minion 12 pt on 16
Cover Art & Design: Nancy de Brouwer, Massive Graphic Design
Paper: Ancient Forest Friendly "Silva" (FSC)—100% post-consumer waste, totally chlorine-free and acid-free

Ronsdale Press wishes to thank the following for their support of its publishing program: the Canada Council for the Arts, the Government of Canada through the Canada Book Fund, the British Columbia Arts Council and the Province of British Columbia through the British Columbia Book Publishing Tax Credit program.

Library and Archives Canada Cataloguing in Publication
Roy, Philip, 1960–, author
  Eco warrior / Philip Roy.

(The Submarine outlaw series; 7)
Issued in print and electronic formats.
ISBN 978-1-55380-347-8 (print)
ISBN 978-1-55380-348-5 (ebook) / ISBN 978-1-55380-349-2 (pdf)

  I. Title. II. Series: Roy, Philip, 1960– . Submarine outlaw series; 7.

PS8635.O91144E26 2015   jC813'.6   C2014-907013-6   C2014-907014-4

At Ronsdale Press we are committed to protecting the environment. To this end we are working with Canopy (formerly Markets Initiative) and printers to phase out our use of paper produced from ancient forests. This book is one step towards that goal.

Printed in Canada by Marquis Printing, Quebec

for Eva

ACKNOWLEDGEMENTS

I wish to express my deepest gratitude to Captain Paul Watson, founder of the Sea Shepherd Society, and lifelong protector of whales, dolphins, and all creatures of the sea. Not only has Captain Watson been a great source of inspiration for the creation of this book, but he has graciously allowed me to include a fictional representation of him, and of the Sea Shepherd Society. It was a generous granting of an ambitious request. It is not often a writer is given the opportunity to fictionalize an active, living hero. It must therefore be emphasized that, though parts of this novel may be based upon real events and characters, the content is fictional, and is the sole responsibility of the author. Captain Watson and the Sea Shepherd Society cannot in any way be held accountable for what is written here.

I must thank Ron and Veronica Hatch for their continued guidance. The books in this series have become increasingly challenging to write, and their commitment to the project has been absolutely steadfast. Thanks also to Meagan, and to Nancy for her cover. I am deeply grateful for the support and guidance of my wife and agent, Leila, whose patience, insight, and energy have kept me on track far more often than I can even remember. I am so fortunate to have the support of my children: Julia, Peter, Thomas, Julian, and Eva, all who weigh in on my projects regularly, and are my greatest source of inspiration. I'd like to also acknowledge my mother, Ellen, and sister, Angela, who generously make me feel my work has good purpose. I must always mention my best friends: Chris, Natasha, and sweet Chiara, whose friendship and home remain my sanctuary. And lastly, I must thank the many readers I meet in schools, shows, and online. The readers of these books have been the richest source of feedback and ideas, and I value their support tremendously.

"We are in a war to save our oceans from ourselves. And if we lose, we all lose because if the oceans die, we all die—it's as simple as that."

— CAPTAIN PAUL WATSON

Chapter One

A HUNDRED YEARS AGO, I would be on my way to World War I. I'd have to lie about my age and say I was eighteen, as a lot of boys did. Then they'd give me a uniform, a rifle, and a gas mask. They'd ship me across the sea with thousands of other recruits, and we'd fight in the trenches of northern France, beside soldiers from other countries. Behind us would be horses, artillery, and ambulances. In front of us would be barbed wire, bullets, and poison gas. We'd huddle in the middle, and fight the best we could.

Probably I'd die, the war would end, and the enemies would become friends again. That's what happens: things go back to how they were before the war began, mostly, until twenty-one years later, when they'd do it all over again in World War II.

Now I'm on my way to a different kind of war. It's complicated. I'm not sure who the enemy is. I'm not sure what the weapons are, or who my allies are, or even how to fight. I only know that I can learn.

This is the war of my time, the war to save the planet.

∞

We were sailing across the Indian Ocean from South Africa to Australia, along one of the least travelled routes in the world. It was mid-afternoon. The sea was choppy but not swelling. The sun was out, and clouds were drifting across the sky from the north. We hadn't seen another vessel in almost a week. Neither had we seen a shark. But we had seen lots of jellyfish, in fact, thousands of them. On the radio I heard a scientist say that when everything else in the sea was dead and gone, there would still be jellyfish.

I had climbed out of the portal onto the hull while the sub was moving at fifteen knots. It wasn't something I normally did, but I wanted to watch the action of the rudder while the sub was sailing, because it seemed to me it was pulling us to starboard. When I examined the rudder at rest, it was fine. I needed to see it in motion.

I was wearing the harness tied to a ten-foot rope. It was an unbreakable rule to wear the harness when the sub was moving, a rule I never disobeyed. The sub was twenty-five feet long, but the distance from the portal to the stern was just slightly more than ten feet. I could reach the stern, but couldn't look over the edge, so I went back inside, untied the harness, and retied it to the next-shortest piece of rope, which was thirty feet. I hesitated for a moment, wondering if I should cut the thirty-foot piece in two, but decided against it. If I fell into the sea, I'd have to pull myself only twenty feet back to the sub, which wasn't far. And chances were, if I fell, I'd grab the rope on my way down anyway, and just pull myself right back up. I was pretty sure of that.

When I reached the stern, I bent one knee to the hull, placed both hands down, and gripped the steel with my fingers—the position a runner takes at the starting line. I peered over the edge. The propeller was churning the water into invisible ribbons. It's funny how you can see movement in water like that, without lines or borders or colours or anything, like waves in the air over a hot road. It was so fascinating for me to watch because I almost never got to see that. To look more closely at the rudder, I shifted my position, putting more weight on my right hand. But as I moved, and took the weight off my left hand for just a second, my right hand slid across the steel on something slippery, like bird droppings, I lost my balance, and, with the movement of the sub, went headfirst into the water.

My immediate thought was to make sure my limbs were clear of the propeller. But that was not a problem because in the two seconds it took to fall, the sub left me five to ten feet behind. Contrary to what I had believed, I did not manage to grab the rope on my way down. The sub was now dragging me behind it like a buoy. No need to panic, I thought, I was attached to the rope with the harness. All I had to do was pull myself back up. But the rope had jammed itself between the rudder and propeller. The moment I reached thirty feet, and the rope grew taut, it went down. In an instant the rope was severed by the propeller, and I was cut adrift.

The full impact of what had just happened didn't hit me right away. I simply assumed I would simply swim back to the hull and climb up. In fact, I didn't even start swimming immediately, but waited for a few seconds, just three or four, to catch my senses. Then, I sprang into action and began to swim. It was tricky, though, because I couldn't swim straight into a spinning propeller, I had to swim to the side of it, which I started to do.

Very quickly I realized I wasn't swimming fast enough— the sub was pulling away from me. So, I shut my eyes and threw everything I had into it. To my utter disbelief, I couldn't seem to gain any distance on the sub. In fact, she kept pulling further away from me.

I swam harder. I swam harder than I had ever swum in all my life. I swam until my lungs were bursting and I was seeing spots. It made no difference; I could not catch her. I stopped swimming because I had to catch my breath, and watched with horror as the sub sailed away.

A wave of emotion rushed up from my stomach into my

eyes, and I was about to burst into tears, but an inner voice interrupted. It was the voice of the sailor I had become over the past two years, the sailor who had sailed around the world, had many close calls, and had always come through. It was the voice of the boy who had learned not to panic, to push fears aside and concentrate on the problem at hand. Surviving a dangerous situation required all of your energy, all of your intelligence, and all of your concentration.

So, I began to analyze the situation. I was a strong swimmer, but was in the middle of the ocean; there was nowhere to swim. I was wearing jeans, a t-shirt, sneakers, and the harness, which was just two strips of wide polyester criss-crossing my torso and waist. I had no flotation devices. I could tread water for maybe a couple of hours—I wasn't really sure how long I could do it if my life depended on it. There were five hours of daylight left. Could I tread water for five hours? But what if I did, and then it turned dark? It would be dark for at least ten hours. Could I . . . no, of course I couldn't! I started to panic. "Stop!" I yelled at myself out loud. "Don't panic!" It was my inner voice again. If I panicked, I was finished. If I panicked, I was dead.

What were the chances I'd get spotted and rescued? Pretty much zero, I figured, though I didn't want to believe that. We hadn't seen a single aircraft since we left South Africa. I felt the ball of panic roll in my stomach again, but forced myself to breathe slowly, and move my arms and legs only as much as necessary to stay afloat. The water was cool, but not cold.

So long as I kept moving, I would stay warm enough . . . for a while. But the risk of hypothermia would grow as my body grew tired. When I became exhausted, I would begin to shiver, which was the body's attempt to retain heat. Eventually the exhaustion would overcome me, and I'd slip beneath the waves and drown. All of these things I knew because I had studied them, and read other people's accounts of being lost at sea.

But some people had survived at sea for remarkably long periods of time, against incredible odds, because they had simply refused to give up. I decided that I would be one of them.

At first, I swung my arms in wide, slow, circular movements, and kicked my legs far in front and back. But my arms kept coming closer to my body, as if protectively, and my movements sped up. I looked up at the sun. The clouds were beginning to cover it in patches. I looked for the sub. I could still see it. On the surface of a calm sea, you can see a whole vessel for about three miles. That is all. Beyond that, it will begin to disappear beneath the horizon. If you are on a ship, or a cliff, or in a lighthouse, you can see much further. When I could no longer see the hull of the sub, I would know it was more than three miles away.

But the sub was difficult to spot in the water anyway. Fully surfaced, the portal rose only four feet above the surface. Another seven feet of submarine lay beneath the surface, with the keel a foot below that. I stared at my watch. It was seventeen minutes after two. I guessed I had been in the water for five minutes already. I forced myself to think: if the sub was moving at fifteen knots, how long would it take to sail three miles? It was hard to concentrate. Part of me was already beginning to wonder what it would be like to die. "Concentrate!" I yelled at myself.

Fifteen knots meant fifteen nautical miles in an hour. A nautical mile was 1.15 regular miles, which was close enough to call it a regular mile for a short distance. If the sub would move fifteen miles in one hour, how long would three miles take? Concentrating hard on the math, I swallowed a mouthful of water. I gagged, and spit it out. "Figure it out!" I yelled. One fifth of an hour, I answered in my mind. One fifth of an hour was . . . twelve minutes. Only twelve minutes? I found that hard to believe. Would the sub begin to go out of sight in just twelve minutes? I searched for it again. I had to raise my head above the choppy waves. There it was. It was smaller but didn't look like it was sinking below the horizon. I looked up at the sun. It was covered by cloud, but I could still see where it was. I stared at my watch. I estimated I had been in the water for seven minutes.

My thoughts turned to my crew. Seaweed, my first mate, was a seagull. The hatch was open. He could climb out and fly away. There was nowhere to fly, but he could find bits of food on the water perhaps, and return to the sub, and rest. I believed he would survive.

Then I thought of Hollie, my second mate. He was just a

small dog. He was safe as long as he stayed inside the sub, where he had food and water for maybe two days. I strained to remember if I had left the storage compartment open or not, where his dog food was. If it were open, he'd have food for more than a month, but no water. So, he would die of thirst. The sub would keep sailing until it ran out of fuel. It was aiming straight for Perth, Australia. If the engine ran non-stop, it would take only a week or so to strike the coast. But if the rudder was pulling it to starboard, as I had suspected, maybe it would miss Australia altogether and sail to Antarctica. Or maybe it would simply go around and around in circles in the Indian Ocean until it ran out of fuel.

Hollie had shown once before that he could climb the ladder by himself, and I imagined that that's what he'd do when I hadn't returned for a long time. He'd jump into the water, and in a short time, he'd drown, too.

My heart sank. I was too young to die. Hollie was too young to die. I knew that this was the risk we had been taking every day since we first went to sea, but I had never minded taking it on Hollie's behalf because I had found him at sea, in a dory, after someone threw him off a wharf with a stone around his neck. I always felt that every day he spent after that was kind of a gift . . . until now. Now, I would feel responsible for his death because I had made a stupid mistake. It was unforgivable. "Stop thinking like that!" I yelled. "If you want to survive, start acting like it!"

I stared at my watch. It was twenty-four minutes after two.

By my estimation, I had been in the water for twelve minutes. If my calculations were correct, the sub should be going out of sight by now. I searched for it. No, there it was. Strangely, it hadn't grown any smaller than it was five minutes earlier. Why was that? I looked at my watch again to make sure. It was twenty-five minutes after two. What was happening? Were my calculations wrong? I started to panic again, so I shut my eyes and took deep breaths until I got it under control. Then I went through the math again. No, twelve minutes was right. I stared at my watch. It was two-thirty. I looked for the sub. There it was, the same size as before. I looked up at the sun. It was slipping out from beneath a cloud, but had moved. No, the sub had moved. Suddenly I realized I was looking at the starboard side of the sub. It was turning. It was sailing in a circle.

Chapter Two

THE FIRST SHIVER JOLTED my body like the shock from an electric fence. It scared me, too, because the water wasn't really that cold. But it *was* colder than my body's temperature, and so, sooner or later, it would bring my temperature down, and there was nothing I could do about it. The harder I worked to keep it up, the faster it would fall.

I checked my watch. It was 2:43. I had been in the water for half an hour. It was surprisingly hard to stay positive. Even if the sub was sailing in a circle, what were my chances of catching her? Pretty small, I figured. I couldn't believe my life had come to this—a couple of years of sailing around the world in a submarine, then one stupid mistake, and my life is over. No one would ever know what had happened to me. I couldn't believe it. I just couldn't.

The sub could only be sailing in a circle because the rope had gotten stuck in the rudder. But how long would it stay there? And if she were cutting a circle, how long would she take to come back to where I was? I tried to remember how to do the math for the circumference of a circle. I was pretty sure it was $2\pi r$, with π being equal to 3.14, and r the radius of a circle. Math was the only thing I was any good at in school; I wasn't great, but good. If the diameter was three miles, then the radius was a mile and a half, so the circumference would be 2 times 3.14, times 1.5, which was almost the same as 3 times 3, which equalled nine. So if the sub were three miles away, and travelling in a perfect circle, she would cover about nine miles in one loop. But how long would that take? If she took an hour for fifteen miles, then nine miles would take her three-fifths as long, or, thirty-six minutes. That meant she should be really close. I raised my head again. Well, she *was* closer, but nowhere near enough for me to catch her. I would have to be right in front of her, or right beside her when she went by, and grab hold of a handle on the side, or pull myself onto the dolphin-shaped nose on the bow. But that was underwater, and would be slippery.

By the time I realized the sub was going to make a pass, and swam as fast as I could towards her, I was too late. She sailed wide of me by about two hundred feet. She wasn't cutting a circle but a spiral, probably because the ocean current was pushing her wide. There was no way I could know if her movement was consistent until the next pass. I could only hope it was, and swim into what I thought was a wider lane. But it was so difficult to know in which direction to swim. There were no land features or buoys or anything to indicate direction, except the sun and the sub, both of which were moving.

I was getting tired. Three more shivers ran up my spine and shook my body. My teeth began to chatter. By the next pass, I would have been in the water for over an hour. If only I were wearing a life jacket, I could pull my arms and legs in close to my body, shut my eyes, and rest. I'd survive so much longer. I needed to rest. Treading water for so long was wasting me.

Then I thought of something. When I was calm, I could hold my breath under water for two minutes. I had trained myself to do that for free diving. So, I started taking deep breaths the way I did before diving, then filled my lungs with air, held my breath, curled up into a ball, and let myself float just beneath the surface. With my lungs full of air I knew I wouldn't sink but would float, like a log. I took a peek at my watch before I went under. I planned to hold my breath for one full minute—slowly counting the seconds in my head, then raise my head out of the water for a few seconds, and do it again. That way I could conserve energy, and hopefully last much longer.

It worked for a while. I still shivered on and off but was able to slow down my pulse, and let my tired limbs rest. The only thing I had to do was watch for the sub coming for her second pass. But an unfortunate consequence of this exercise was that it made me dizzy after a while, and I had to take breaks from holding my breath so long. I used those breaks to search for the sub, and tried to gauge her position on the curve, which was difficult to do. In fact, I was really just guessing.

About halfway through the second loop, I had a visitor. Seaweed climbed the portal, jumped into the air, and flew over to me. It was so easy for him. He flew over my head, hovered for a few seconds, and then landed beside me. I felt emotional to see him. I cried. I couldn't help it. We had been through so much together. I spoke to him, and told him how much I admired him. I realized as I spoke out loud, that I didn't really believe I was going to make it. I would never give up, of course, but I knew my chances of surviving were very small. Seeing Seaweed reminded me that Hollie might also climb out, especially once he saw Seaweed leave, and that worried me tremendously.

"Go back, Seaweed! Go back and find Hollie. Go find Hollie, Seaweed!"

He wouldn't leave, so I splashed water at him until he took off. I watched him fly away and land on the sub, which seemed awfully close now. She was coming again! I started swimming. But I was so tired, and my limbs were stiff, and I couldn't swim very fast. There was no way I could make it.

Once again the sub passed a few hundred feet away from me, and this time I saw Hollie on the hull. He had climbed out, and was clutching the hull with his paws, searching the sea for me. When he spotted me, he jumped into the water and started to swim my way. I felt so sad. I didn't even know if he could make it all the way. If he turned back, he would never catch the sub, couldn't climb onto her anyway, and would drown for sure. As tired as I was, I started swimming towards him, and kept calling to him to encourage him to keep swimming towards me. Hollie was a good swimmer but he was so small, and the choppiness was hard for him. He had to hold his head high to be able to see where he was going.

Once again I cried when I was united with one of my crew. But this time it was tragic because I knew that Hollie could never go back. He had to stay with me. He could not tread water; he could only swim, and I was too tired now to hold onto him for long. I couldn't escape the reality that the end was near for both of us.

Hollie scratched at my face with his paws. He was looking for a place to rest. We looked into each other's eyes, and I wondered if he understood. I didn't think he did, or perhaps he simply wasn't accepting it. Something about that look in his eyes inspired me in an odd way. I didn't really understand it but felt it. He simply wasn't giving up. So I shouldn't, either.

I pulled off the harness, tied it around Hollie, and then tied it around my neck, as tightly as I could stand it. Now, I was wearing him on the back of my neck, with his front and back paws hanging down on either side, so that they couldn't scratch me. He could have wrestled free if he wanted to, but he seemed to understand that this was his only chance to rest. He was used to being carried on my back in the tool bag.

But how long could I hold on? Hollie didn't weigh much, but my movement was more restricted now, and I couldn't hold my breath and roll into a ball to rest. One advantage, however, was that Hollie was warming me up. I decided to swim slowly but steadily towards a wider lane, and just hope somehow the sub would pass close enough to us.

The next half hour passed as if it were an eternity. Every second was difficult. I was so deeply exhausted I could have just let go and sunk beneath the waves. Part of me wanted to do that, just to rest. It was Hollie who kept me going. I swam so slowly, doing the breaststroke and barely kicking my feet. Eventually we saw the sub. But the only reason we saw her was because Seaweed was standing on top of the hatch. She was so close! My heart started beating fast. I could not miss this chance.

But I was too stiff and restricted to swim. And so, as the sub drew near, I untied the harness, and set Hollie free. I had to try to catch the sub first, and then rescue him after. It was our only chance.

The sub came towards me like a shark, straight and fast. I swam as hard as I could, and tried to get right in front of her. But it was so difficult to gauge. I swam forward, then back, and then forward again. Hollie followed me. I focused on Seaweed. Suddenly, the sub was here. She struck me on the shoulder, and started pushing me under, but I reached up as she went over me, and my hand slid across the side of the hull until I felt a handle, and I squeezed it with all my strength. I shut my eyes, and let the sub pull me through the water. I couldn't believe I had caught her. My sense of relief was overwhelming. But I had to climb up and get inside as fast as possible, come around, and find Hollie before he drowned. He must have thought I had abandoned him.

It was so hard to climb up. I had nothing left, and could barely do it without falling. All I wanted was to cling to the handles and rest, and just let the sub drag me through the water. But if I did, Hollie would drown. So I reached for the next handle, and the next, until I was on top of the hull. I was dizzy with exhaustion, but couldn't stop there.

When I saw Seaweed, I told him to search for Hollie. "Go find Hollie, Seaweed!" I shouted desperately. I pointed behind us. "Go find Hollie!" This was something I knew he would do. He jumped into the air. Then I pulled myself onto the portal and went down inside. When I reached the wheel, I turned the sub around and went back. I found Hollie swimming in small circles, with Seaweed next to him, squawking at him to stay afloat.

Hollie swam towards the sub as soon as he saw her. He was beginning to fail. I put the sub in reverse for a few seconds to cut our drift, then shut the engine. I climbed back out, jumped into the water, and met Hollie at the bottom handle on the side. Together we clung to the hull and rested.

"I am sorry, Hollie. I am sorry."

He looked at me with an understanding only animals have. He did not blame me for the mistake.

Chapter Three

I NEVER KNEW GRATITUDE was something you could feel in your fingertips. When I climbed into the portal with Hollie in my arms, the mere touch of the ladder filled me with such thankfulness that I wept for joy. The warmth inside, the dryness, and the familiarity of all of our things, overwhelmed me with such happiness that my eyes kept welling up. I had thought we were dead.

Hollie was exhausted. He must have swallowed sea water, too, because he threw up a couple of times, and made a wheezing noise with his breathing for about an hour or so. He went straight to his blanket, plopped down, and began cleaning himself, which was a big job because he was soaked through and through. I wondered if he felt I had abandoned him. If he did, he didn't show it.

Seaweed didn't know what all the fuss was about, but happily gobbled down a handful of extra dog biscuits that I gave him for being such a great first mate. Without him, Hollie and I wouldn't have survived.

Slowly and stiffly I dried myself off, changed my clothes, and warmed myself up. But my limbs were still shaking like a wind-up toy. It was nervousness. When you think you are going to die, your body goes on high alert, and it takes a long time to calm down afterward. I made a large pot of tea, and sweetened it with canned milk and brown sugar. My hands trembled as I drank it. I couldn't seem to stop shaking. I put on a pot of beans, and broke hard cakes into it. While I ate, I looked around the sub with awe. My life was richer than I ever realized before. I mean, I knew I was very lucky to have what I had—my own submarine, the freedom to travel around the world, and two very special friends as my crew. It wasn't that I had taken that for granted before. I hadn't. But having come so close to losing it all, it felt as though I were really seeing it for the first time. It was such a strange feeling.

But as my belly filled with beans and hot tea, my limbs began to feel like lead, and my head started to droop, and I barely made it to my hanging cot before falling face down and instantly to sleep.

I slept as if I had been drugged. It was the longest sleep I ever had at sea. Had I known it would be so long I would have sealed the hatch and submerged a couple of hundred feet in case another vessel came by. I always trusted myself to wake to the sound of the radar beeping, but might not have this time, though the chances we'd get hit by a passing ship in the middle of the Indian Ocean were probably less than the chances of getting struck by lightning. Besides, I preferred to leave Seaweed free to come and go. I knew that Hollie would never climb the portal while I was inside the sub, especially when he was so exhausted.

When I went to sleep, the engine was off, and the sub was free to drift with the current, which had been flowing at about three knots in a southerly direction, towards Antarctica, when I last checked. But the current was always changing. It was 5,432 miles from Cape Town, South Africa, to Perth, Australia, along the southerly side of the Indian Ocean. Sailing as the crow flies, at eighteen knots, for fifteen hours a day, it should have taken us eighteen days. But that was kind of a joke, because the sea doesn't lie around like the land; it keeps moving, like the wind. If we were sailing at eighteen knots, and the current was flowing against us at three, as it often was, and the wind was pushing us back at four, then we were really only making eleven knots. And if the current was swinging us north and south, and the waves were tossing us up and down like a yo-yo, then we were not sailing as the crow flies, but more the way a dog might wander through the woods, which might be only six or seven knots, and take us fifty-four days, which I sure hoped it didn't.

When I woke, twenty hours later, I could tell from the still-ness inside that there was no wind outside, and the sea was perfectly calm, which was extremely rare in the middle of an ocean. Curious, I picked up Hollie, who was wagging his tail at my feet, and we climbed the portal for a look. Boy, were we in for a surprise. Not only were there no wind or waves, the sea was brown and murky, as if a meteorite had fallen from the sky and scorched it. For a moment I wondered if I was dreaming. But I wasn't. There was a thick film of algae float-ing on the surface, like a layer of mud, and the sun was flat and white. I couldn't believe the strangeness of it. Usually the sea reflects the sky, but sometimes the sky will reflect the sea. Bewildered, I lay my head down on top of Hollie's head, and we just stared. Everything was so quiet. The sea lay as still and brown as a bowl of chocolate milk.

Was this a dead zone? Dead zones were created when fer-tilizers and poisons were washed out to sea by rivers. They formed pools of water so toxic nothing could live in them. I had never seen one before. Was this one of those? It smelled like pepper and stinky sneakers. Did dead zones drift so far from land? I had no idea.

As Hollie and I stared at the strangely brown horizon, I heard the radar beep for the first time in ten days. I climbed down the ladder and went to the screen. There was a vessel ten miles east of us, but it was not moving. That seemed a bit odd. Why would a vessel be sitting still in the middle of the Indian Ocean, unless, like us, her crew was sleeping? That was certainly possible, and yet, I couldn't help feeling a little nervous about it, perhaps because of the close call we had just had. So I decided to submerge to periscope depth, motor closer on battery power, and take a peek at her before she had a chance to see us.

But I had to fix the rudder first. And so, with the sub sitting still, I climbed onto the hull, lay down, and looked over the stern. The rope was still wedged between the rudder and the arm that supported it. If it hadn't jammed there when I fell, the sub would not have cut such a small circle, and we would not be alive now. When I pulled the rope free, I discovered a piece of hard wire beneath it. I had no idea where it came from, or how it got there, but it must have been the reason for the slight turn to starboard. The rudder itself was un-damaged.

I went back inside, flipped the dive switch, engaged the batteries, and heard the hatch shut and seal just as we slipped beneath the surface. I breathed a sigh of relief. How I loved the stealth of a submarine.

I looked again at the radar screen. Why was the vessel not moving? Was she a fishing boat? But there were no fish out here; it was too deep. Was she a research vessel studying dead zones? Maybe. Or, was she an abandoned ship, drifting around in the strangely circular currents of the Indian Ocean for years and years? I had read about such ships. They were rare but they did exist. Our sub had almost become one of them. On the other hand, she might be just a container fallen off a ship, or a sea mine, or a piece of garbage with metal, being picked up by radar. She could have been any of those things. We had seen them all.

As we drew closer, I raised the periscope, but couldn't see anything yet. She wasn't very big, whatever she was. Hollie lifted his head from the corner, sniffed, and listened.

"Might just be garbage, Hollie. Might be nothing."

He wagged his tail and dropped his head onto his blanket. He was feeling much better now, and would give anything for a walk on a beach. Seaweed was in a deep slumber on the other side of the observation window. Sometimes he slept so deeply you'd think he was hibernating. But if I opened a bag of cookies, or dog biscuits, he'd be on his feet in an instant.

From five miles I spotted the mast of a small sailboat sticking out of the water. At three miles, I saw the whole boat. She was just sitting there, like an old hen, kind of sad and lonely. Why she looked sad and lonely, I wasn't sure, except that her sail was down, and she had a defeated look about her, though not distress. I couldn't really say what the difference was, but you could feel it. A vessel in distress is looking for help, and you can sense it. I never got the feeling that this vessel was doing that. From a mile away, I saw a hulking man at the wheel. But what a strange man he was. It was hot out, and yet he was wearing a heavy coat, hat, and beard. He was hunched over the wheel as if steering through a storm. But there wasn't even a breath of wind. That was very odd.

On the bow, I saw another man in a dark wool sweater, rubber boots, and cap. Both men had to be melting in this

heat. Maybe they were like the old fishermen of Newfoundland, who wore heavy work clothes and long underwear right
through the warmest days of summer. But this wasn't Newfoundland; this was the middle of the Indian Ocean! It looked
pretty crazy to me. And there was something else strange
about the sailor on the bow, in the way he was slouched over.
He looked seasick. He was bent over a bucket. But how could
he be seasick when there were no waves? Besides, they were
both seasoned sailors from the look of them.

It looked so strange, and I stared for so long that suddenly
I didn't have enough time to turn without creating a big fat
wave, which would have come out of nowhere, slapped them
on the side, and told them there was something big in the
water. Instead, I hit the dive switch again, and we went right
underneath them. They would have felt our wake still, though
not as much, and seen our bubbles, if they had been looking
over the side. At the last second, as I pulled the periscope beneath the surface, I saw a figure in a white sheet burst out of
the cabin and float along the deck. Oh boy.

Chapter Four

I STEERED SHARPLY TO starboard, swung around 180 degrees, shut off the batteries, and pumped enough air into the tanks to rise back to periscope depth. We drifted to a stop about seventy-five feet from the bow of the sailboat. Up close, everything looked very different. Those weren't sailors on deck, those were mannequins! They were made of wood, and were as stiff as stone. Their clothes hung on their bodies like towels on drying racks. And the figure in white was just an old woman with long white hair and a flowing white shirt. When she moved quickly, her shirt trailed behind her like a sheet. She went all around the deck looking over the side into the water. She knew something had passed beneath her. Her boat was tossing gently now. I waited. I wanted to know who else was on board.

After ten minutes, no one else came out of the cabin, so I pumped more air into the tanks and surfaced. We came up slowly. I didn't want to scare her. She was still looking over the side when I opened the hatch and she turned and saw me. I couldn't tell if she was frightened, or just really surprised. I waved. She stared harder. After a few seconds, she broke into a smile, and waved back.

"Jumpin' Jucifer! Who the heck are you?" Her voice was dry and raspy, but I could hear her all right.

"My name is Alfred."

"Well, my name is Margaret. Where are you from?"

"Newfoundland."

"And where is that?"

"In Canada. Just a second." Hollie was whining at the bottom of the ladder so I climbed down and picked him up. Seaweed squeezed past us, hopped up the ladder, and jumped into the air. When we came back up, the woman's eyes were bigger than before.

"Young man, a seagull just flew out of your submarine!"

"I know. That's my first mate." Seaweed was already beginning to circle in the air. He would wind slowly around and around because there was no wind to give him lift. It would take him about half an hour to rise until he was just a tiny dot in the sky above us, only to discover nothing but water for as far as he could see. Then he'd come back down.

"And the little dog, is that your second mate?"

"Yes. This is Hollie."

"Are there any more?"

"No. Just us. Is there anyone else on your boat?"

"Just Brutus and Clive." She pointed towards the manne-quins. "They keep the pirates and bogeyman away. What's your name again?"

"Alfred."

"Alfred, I'm Margaret."

She had already told me that. We stared in awkward silence for a moment.

"Why don't you come over for tea, Alfred?" she said.

"Okay."

"Okay then."

So I motored closer, tossed a line, and she tied it up. She was pretty able for someone who looked older than my grandfather. Her sailboat was made of wood, and was about twenty-five feet long, the same size as the sub. The deck was low and the cabin deep, so that waves would wash over the entire thing without rolling her. She was built for ocean voy-ages, not just for day trips along a coastline. But she was old. A sturdy railing wrapped the deck, and I wondered how many times Margaret had been thrown against it in bad weather. She was the oldest person I had ever seen at sea, but she didn't look feeble. As soon as we stepped on board, Hollie wriggled free, and she caught him and scooped him up. Now that I could see the mannequins up close, I couldn't believe I had been so easily fooled. "I thought they were real."

"The most useful men I've ever known, these two. I found them in an alley behind a shop in Melbourne, a few years ago. I knew they were the right blokes for me straight away. Of course I've had to buy each a new set of clothes, and give them beards, but they've turned out all right. They're nothing to feed. But let me look at this little doggie. What did you say his name was?"

"Hollie."

Margaret looked affectionately into Hollie's eyes. He liked her right away.

"How long have you been stuck here in the doldrums?"

"The doldrums? Is that what you call it? I was thinking it was just a meditation. Doesn't it look like the sea is meditating?"

I glanced around. It looked like the doldrums to me. "Did you run out of fuel?"

"Well, I suppose I did, considering that the wind is my fuel." She put her nose to Hollie's nose. "Yes, I'd say we ran out of fuel. But then, we weren't going anywhere anyway, were we, cutie-pie? And now that I've got you here, I think I'll eat you up." And she cradled Hollie in her arms like a baby.

"You must be going somewhere?"

"Nope. This is it. I have arrived. Doesn't this look like the end of the world to you?"

She had a point, but I didn't know how to answer that so I just followed her inside, sat down at her table, and looked around while she boiled a pot of water. There wasn't much to see. The sun came in through the door and windows, so that it was almost as bright inside as on deck. She had some photographs thumbtacked to the walls of her cupboards, but they were curled up so much you couldn't see the people in them. She had piles of books on the floor and on her bed, which wasn't in a separate room. Her cabin was just one large open space, with a few smaller compartments in the stern, like my sub. But she had a real kitchen with a table bolted to the floor, and she had a fridge and stove. I noticed that the fridge door wasn't shut, and there appeared to be books inside. Then I realized that she had boiled the pot of water on a small one-burner hotplate hooked up to a propane tank, instead of her stove. She had no electricity because she had no fuel to run an engine or a generator. There were a couple of packs of playing cards on the table, and they were worn ragged. She must have played a lot of solitaire. I wondered if she was lonely.

She took the water from a plastic barrel. Rainwater. Hollie was cradled in one of her arms like a football. He didn't mind. She looked thoughtful, as though she were turning something over in her mind. When the water started to boil, she raised the pot and poured two cups. She turned off the stove, put the pot down, took two tea bags out of a jar, and dropped them into the cups, all the while holding Hollie under her arm. Then she put powdered milk, sugar, and spoons on the table. The tea smelled slightly stale, but it was nice to have someone else serve me a cup.

"Are you sailing to Australia?" she asked.

"Yes."

"Why?"

"I want to help save the oceans. I was told that Australia is the best place to learn how to become an environmentalist."

She stopped, and stared at me with wonder. "Are you serious?"

"Yes."

She broke into a strange laugh, which almost sounded like a witch's cackle. "Most boys your age just want to chase girls. You want to save the world. That's amazing."

"The oceans are dying. I want to make them healthy again."

"Indeed they are. But are you the sort of young man who likes to hear the truth, or do you just like to hear happy endings?" She squinted at me.

"I like to hear the truth."

"Yes, I can see that you do. Well then, I'm sorry to be the one to have to tell you, but I think that you're about thirty years too late."

"What?"

"You can't save the oceans now. Nobody can. It's too late."

The way she stood in front of the little stove, by an open window, we might have been in any old shack in Newfoundland. "Oh, you might save a few turtles, dolphins, or whales, but you can't stop the poisoning of the sea. And you can't stop global warming. It's too late for that. We crossed that line a long time ago."

She stared with ice-cold eyes and a severe face. Then, like butter melting in a pan, her face changed. She became more sympathetic. Her eyes turned glossy, and she spoke as if she were apologizing to me personally. "I don't think we were ever meant to survive, you know, as a species. We seem to have been born with a special talent to destroy. It's what we do best."

I took a drink of my tea. Then I put more sugar in it. "But . . . there are lots of people trying to make things better. Lots of people want to save the Earth." My voice came out a little higher than I wanted it to be.

"True enough. But for every person who cares, a thousand don't. That's the problem, don't you see? And we can't keep up with our own destructiveness. We cause environmental disasters every single day. Do you read the papers?"

"I listen to the radio."

"Then you know what I say is true. Do they tell you how we've stopped drilling for oil, burning coal, and making weapons? Is that what they say?"

"No."

"Do they tell you how we've cut carbon emissions, are saving endangered animals, and are no longer making war?"

"No."

"You see? And the Earth just can't take it anymore." Her face changed again. She relaxed and smiled as if the bad news was over. Now she seemed like a grandmother. She reached into a cupboard and pulled down a chocolate bar.

Her movements were a little shaky. "I keep this for special oc- casions," she said warmly. She pulled on a pair of glasses with Coke-bottle lenses. Her eye sockets were deep, her cheekbones high, and the skin on her bones thin. But her hair, even though it was silver and white, was wild and full of life. She reminded me of an eagle. Her face was sharp like that, and her hands long and bony, like talons. She broke the chocolate in half, and then broke the halves into smaller chunks. "But good for you that you want to save the world! What a noble pursuit. How I wish it weren't so darned hopeless."

"But . . . I don't think it's hopeless. I think there's always hope." My voice sounded high, like a girl's.

"Of course you do, dear. You're a young man. You're sup- posed to be full of hope. Where would the world be if young people didn't have hope? Would you like some chocolate?"

"Yes, thank you."

"Good." She pushed the plate of broken pieces across the table. "We're not the first species to go extinct, you know."

Chapter Five

MARGARET'S WORDS WEIGHED heavily on me, but I was determined to stay positive. "Can I look at the engine?"

"You want to look at the engine? Well, I suppose you can. I don't know if it works, but you can look at it."

I opened up the main compartment in the stern, and found books, dishes, bags of clothing, and sleeping bags all stuffed around and underneath the engine. I could tell right away it hadn't been used in years because of the way it was packed. It couldn't breathe.

"Can I pull all this stuff out?"

"There's stuff in there?"

"Yah."

"Oh, yes, pull it out. We can always put it back. I didn't know there was . . . Oh! Look at that! I had forgotten about those clothes. Look here! Books! Oh! *Silent Spring!*" She held the book close to her heart as if it were an old friend. "Rachel Carson died of cancer right after she wrote this book to warn the world of the dangers of pesticides. It was the first one of its kind. If you're going to become an environmentalist, you'll want to read this book." She handed it to me. "What a brave woman she was. Look, here's a copy of *Walden*. Have you read Thoreau, Alfred?"

"I don't think so."

"You'd know if you did." When she stared at me with her glasses on, her eyes looked twice as big. "You must read Thoreau, Alfred. He was the father of the environmental movement. I don't see how anyone can become an environmentalist if they don't read Thoreau. I bet you'd find you've got many things in common." She handed me the book. "Here, take these books with you. It won't make any difference to the world now, but it sure will make a difference in your own life. Everybody should read Thoreau."

I put the books under my arm. "Thank you. Would you mind if I tried to start the engine? I'm curious to see if it still works. I'll have to get some things from my sub first."

Margaret frowned. All the pleasantness washed out of her face. "Well, I don't see the point, really. But if you must, I won't stop you. You do see the irony of starting an engine to go out and save a world that is dying because of people burning too many engines though, don't you?" She examined me so closely I felt like a bug.

"Yes, but . . ."

"It seems to me your time would be much better spent reading these books than starting another engine. Aren't there enough engines running in the world?" She stood with her hands on her hips and a kind of impatient look on her face. I didn't want to be rude, but I really wanted to see if I could get the engine running. What if she got caught in a terrible storm? She was crazy to be at sea without fuel and a proper working engine.

"The man who sold me the boat told me that everything worked just fine. But that was seven years ago. I don't know if it works now."

"You mean you've *never* used it?" I couldn't believe it.

"No."

"But . . . how do you get in and out of port?"

"Very slowly. They hate me when I come into ports. I don't know why everyone's in such a hurry. Isn't that the point of sailing?"

Oh boy. They must have really hated her. In a busy port, she would have gotten in everyone's way. "How long have you been at sea?"

"Seven years, on and off. I went to sea for the first time when I turned seventy-one. I didn't know a thing about it. I was looking at retirement condos one day when I saw an old man in a sailboat. If that man could do it, I said to myself, then so could I. So I sold my house and car and all my furniture, took a sailing course, and bought this boat. It was the smartest thing I ever did."

"Don't you get lonely?"

"Nope."

"Aren't you afraid at sea, alone?"

"Are you?"

"No."

"Then why should I be? Somewhere along the way I passed the point of being afraid. I've already lived longer than I ever expected to. We're all terminal, Alfred. Here would be as good a place to go as any, don't you think?"

I raised my head over the bags of clothing to look at her face. I realized I couldn't tell when she was joking and when she wasn't. Maybe she was never joking. I really didn't know.

"If a bad storm comes, I think you'll be glad to have a working engine."

"I've been through plenty a storm, let me tell you. I just tie everything down and go to sleep." She raised her eyebrows. Man, she was stubborn. But I supposed she had to be.

"I'll be right back. Can I leave Hollie here?"

"You sure can. You can leave him with me and pick him up on your way back to Newfoundland."

Now she was joking. I mean, I thought she was. I went back to the sub, filled the tool bag with a can of oil, an assortment of tools, and a plastic tarp, and hung it over my shoulder. Then I picked up one of the portable tanks of diesel. It was so heavy I had to make a separate trip for it, and carry it with both hands. Getting it up the ladder was really tough. If I hadn't been doing chin-ups every day for the past two years, I probably wouldn't have been able to lift it out by myself. But I managed. When I climbed out, Seaweed was there to greet me.

"Hey, Seaweed." He stared at the can and twisted his head. He wasn't impressed. He had just learned that there was no land. That meant no beaches with dead carcasses to tear apart, or crabs to attack and eat. I knew he would explore Margaret's boat for food though, and that's what he did next. He took a hop and landed on her cabin. "Good luck with that, Seaweed." I dragged the fuel over.

As I expected, there was no oil in the engine, either. The whole thing would need a flushing and a tune up, but before I could even consider doing that, I needed to know if it would start. So, I poured in a little oil, and let it seep into the engine. It was a small, old, two-stroke diesel motor, the kind that runs forever and is easy to fix. I emptied the whole tank of diesel into the tank. That was a bit sneaky. I wanted to know that she had enough fuel to ride out a storm, whether she planned to use it or not.

"That stinks!" said Margaret, and she went out on deck with Hollie.

"It will go away," I said, "after a while."

"I sure am glad Brutus and Clive don't play around with engines."

Now was she being serious? She sure sounded serious. If

she was, that meant she was crazy for sure. But then I thought of my grandfather's sense of humour, if you could call it that, and realized that she must have been joking. Maybe really old people just didn't care anymore if you thought they were funny or not.

I greased the engine everywhere that I could. It had nice brass fittings. It would look really beautiful cleaned up and polished. Margaret had protected it from the salt without knowing it by wrapping it so tightly with plastic bags. I spun the flywheel. It turned easily enough. That was a good sign. Once the fuel and oil had settled in, I tried igniting the engine. Nothing. I tapped the starter gently with a wrench and tried again. Nothing. I tapped it a little harder and tried again. This time the engine coughed a little, like an old troll waking up under a bridge. *"Cough . . . cough . . . cough . . . cough . . . chug . . . chug . . . chug, chug, chug, chug, chug, chug, chug, chug . . ."* Awesome!

"Alfred! There's a cloud of blue smoke out here! It's horrible! Turn the darned thing off! You're killing the environment!"

I poked my head outside. "Please just give it a minute. It's burning old oil. The blue smoke will go away in a minute. But I really should clean the engine. Do you mind if I do that? It would take a day or two."

Margaret made a fussy face. "I don't see the point, Alfred. I'm not planning on using it. You'd just be wasting your time."

"It would be good practice for me, actually."

"I won't use it."

Gosh she was stubborn. "Do you mind if I do it anyway?"

"Don't you have to get to Australia to save the world?"

She was losing her patience. But I felt stubborn, too. I didn't want to leave her without fuel and a working engine. Maybe she was ready to throw in the towel, I didn't know, but I wouldn't be part of that. My newfound gratitude for life made me very determined.

"One or two days shouldn't make too much difference."

"Oh, suit yourself!" She went to the bow with Hollie, and sat down.

So, I got to work. I shut off the engine, drained the oil, and flushed the engine with diesel fuel. Then, I left it to dry. I sprayed lubricating and anti-rust oil everywhere there were moving parts that could be loosened, tightened, or removed, and let it sit. I took fine steel wool and buffed the rust from the casing and driveshaft as well as I could. It was a small engine, and it didn't take two whole days for that much work, but it took a whole day for everything to dry and the oil to work its magic.

Once it was dry, I tightened everything up again, filled the engine with oil, and snuck in another can of fuel for the tank. It was slow, steady, relaxing work. While I kept at it, Margaret and I chatted. Usually she was out on deck, and I was inside, and we talked without seeing each other, except when she got worked up over something. Then, she'd come in and stand in the doorway to the cabin with her hands on her hips, and wait for me to make eye contact, such as when I suggested that she didn't have to be so negative, that it wasn't too late, there was still time to save the oceans and the world. I had my head buried beneath the engine when she stood in front of the light and darkened my view.

"The reason we are in the mess we are in is because humans are greedy and thoughtless, Alfred. They want bigger cars, bigger houses, bigger steaks, bigger toys, and they don't care how they get them. They don't want anyone digging, cutting, or burning in their own backyard, but they sure as heck don't mind someone digging, cutting, or burning in somebody else's backyard, just so long as they don't have to see it. And if people on the other side of the world are dying in war or drought, that's just fine so long as they can have their oil, coal, and all their consumer goods. But what humans haven't realized in all this time is that we're all connected. We're all connected to each other, and to the Earth, and to every other living creature. What one creature does affects everybody else. That's a lesson we should have learned from aboriginal peoples a long time ago, but didn't, and now it's too late."

I raised my head. "Aboriginal peoples?"

"Yes, Aboriginal peoples, because they have a healthier relationship with the Earth. They only take what they need, and they give back. Aboriginal peoples tend to be self-sufficient and naturally sustaining, when left to their own devices. They've learned to be that way over thousands of years. Then we come along with our industrial revolution, and we just can't use up the Earth's resources fast enough. We don't care how garbage piles up. We don't care if we poison rivers and lakes and oceans. And even when it's evident that it's too late, as it is now, people still don't care so long as they can get to the store to buy something else. The last gallon of gas is probably going to be burned up in the tank of some guy on his way to a dealership to buy a new truck!" She stood behind the bags of clothing with her arms folded like a wrestler. There was a slight breeze now, and it came inside and lifted her hair off her shoulders. The weather was changing. "We're the most destructive creature that ever crawled out from underneath a rock. It's a wonder there's anything still alive. Do you know who's going to inherit the Earth?"

"Who?"

"Jellyfish!"

"Oh."

Chapter Six

BY THE SECOND DAY, the sea had changed. It was choppy once again, and the brown algae had disappeared, probably because we had drifted away from it. Now, a grey sea reflected a grey sky. I wondered how comfortable Margaret would be in a choppy sea. One glance at her walking along the deck told me it made no difference to her whatsoever. She was the seasoned sailor I had thought Brutus and Clive were.

By the middle of the day, I was finished with the engine. It was topped up with oil, and I had put enough fuel in her tank to allow her to travel maybe five hundred miles. It was a small motor, and wouldn't propel her anywhere in a hurry, but she wouldn't have to stay in the middle of a storm, either. And something told me there was one coming. After two years at sea, I could tell. I wondered if Margaret could.

"We've drifted out of the doldrums."

"Or perhaps they have drifted out of us?"

"What?"

She smiled, but it wasn't as warm as before. And I sensed that she was agitated about something. "You'd better get on your way now, Alfred. You've got a world to save." She made more effort to smile this time. I turned and looked at the horizon. There was definitely bad weather coming. The sea in the east was rougher than in the west.

"Maybe I should leave in the morning."

"But you've done everything that you wanted to do. Why would you stay until morning?"

"I think there's a storm coming."

"So what if there is? Do you think you have to stay around and protect me?"

"It's what I'd do for anybody else."

"Yes, I'm sure that it is. But what if I don't want someone to protect me? What if I want to face the storm by myself, as I am used to doing? What then?"

Her words sounded unfriendly, but I didn't think she meant them to be. She was still smiling at me, if awkwardly, and speaking in a friendly tone. She simply didn't want my help. She wanted to look after herself. I knew I should have understood that because I was exactly the same way. If I hadn't almost drowned a few days ago I probably would have found it easier to accept. "You don't want me to stay?"

"No. I am perfectly able to look after myself. Just like you. Maybe you look at me and see an old woman, but I can assure you I can look after myself just as well as you can. I think maybe we're cut from the same cloth, Alfred—both of us sailing around the world by ourselves. You should be able to understand me better than anybody else, don't you think?"

"I guess so. If that's what you want."

"It is. There's just one thing I'd like to ask of you."

"What's that?"

"Have you got any books that I haven't read, that you wouldn't mind parting with?"

"I don't know. I'll show you what I have."

So I went in, grabbed all my books, and carried them out. It wasn't a very big collection. Margaret looked them over quickly. "Read it, read it, read it . . . Oh! The *Bhagavad Gita*! Oh, that's fabulous! I've always wanted to read it, and never got around to it. Do you think you could part with this?"

"Sure. You can have it." I was glad I had something that she wanted.

"Thank you."

The wind was beginning to howl now, and swells were raising and dropping the boat.

"I'm going to tie everything down now and get cosy in my bed. You had really better get going, Alfred. Please give your doggie and seagull a hug for me, will you?" She had to speak loudly now to be heard over the wind. If the severity of a storm could be measured by how quickly it blew in, then I'd have said we were in for a bad one, but I didn't honestly know if that were true.

"Are you absolutely certain you don't want me to stay around till morning?"

"I am absolutely certain. Goodbye, Alfred. It was a real pleasure meeting you." Margaret shot out her hand. I reached over and shook it. Her hand was bony, but strong.

"Good luck to you!" she said. Now, she was smiling warmly again, and seemed almost glad the storm was coming. "You'd better go."

"Okay." I took a few steps towards the railing. The sub and boat were starting to bang against each other. I turned around again. Margaret waved. "Goodbye!"

Her voice was swallowed up by the wind. I waved back, then untied the rope, climbed over the railing, and jumped onto the hull of the sub. From the portal, I watched her toss a sea anchor over the bow, then lift heavy coils of rope, and drop them overboard. That was smart. The sea anchor was a heavy nylon bag that would sit at the end of a couple of hundred feet of rope, and keep the bow pointed into the waves and wind, so that the boat wouldn't turn sideways and swamp. She knew what she was doing. I waved one more time, but she was too busy to look my way. It would soon be dark. I took a final glance at Brutus and Clive before I shut the hatch, climbed down the ladder, and joined Hollie and

Seaweed inside. Reluctantly, I let water into the tanks and we began to submerge.

But we didn't go anywhere. I had agreed to leave Margaret's boat, but she couldn't make us leave the area. Nor could she know we were still here, just a hundred feet directly below her. But we were. I fed the crew, made myself a cup of tea, sat on my bed, and opened the book by Thoreau. I tried to read for an hour, but was so sleepy it was hard to concentrate. I kept reading the same sentences over and over. Then I lay down and shut my eyes. I only intended to take a nap.

Seven hours later, I woke. It was perfectly quiet inside the sub, except for Hollie's soft breathing, and the occasional ruffling of Seaweed's feathers. Above us, I knew a storm was raging. I wondered how bad it was. I wondered how Margaret was doing. Should I go up and check? Would she be angry if I did? Hollie saw me raise my head, and he came over.

"What should we do, Hollie? Go up and check on Margaret, or wait?"

Hollie raised his paw. I picked him up and let him sit on my bed. "We can go up and just take a peek through the periscope. She won't even know we are here. She's probably sleeping anyway. What do you think?"

I looked into his eyes. Hollie was the sweetest dog that ever lived. And he was, without question, a rescuer.

"Okay, let's take a peek."

I pumped air into the tanks and we began to rise. Halfway up, I felt the storm. It was a bad one for sure. I raised the periscope before surfacing, but the waves prevented me from seeing anything. We would have to surface, and I'd have to strap on the harness even before opening the hatch. Chances were Margaret had drifted, even though her sea anchor would have slowed her drift. What I was counting on was picking up her signal on radar from the crests of the swells.

But there was no signal. And even after twenty minutes there was no signal. Nothing. Where was she? I climbed the ladder and opened the hatch. The wind screamed like a witch, and the rain pounded sideways against me. The sea was so wild it was impossible to make a sighting. I carried up the binoculars and scanned the darkness for any sign of a light, but couldn't see anything but dark walls of water rising and falling. It was hopeless. Margaret was gone. But where? I didn't think she would have drifted out of our radar range so quickly, not with a sea anchor in the water. Had she sunk? I forced the thought out of my mind. Was it possible she had started the engine after all, and was motoring out of the storm? How could I know? Would I ever know?

Chapter Seven

TWO WEEKS LATER, we reached Perth. After a month at sea, the sight of land brought tears to my eyes. I couldn't help it. I was so used to seeing nothing but water I forgot just how much I missed the land. When I caught my first glimpse of it—just a thin flat line on the horizon—my eyes flooded with tears. That we had almost died on the way here probably had something to do with it.

Hollie's nose was twitching all the time now. He was picking up new smells through the open hatch, and wouldn't leave my side for fear I might go for a walk without him. If I went to the stern to check the engine, he had to come with me. If I went up the ladder, he sat at the bottom and whined pitifully until I came back down.

"Don't worry, Hollie. I won't go for a walk without you, I promise."

Seaweed knew there was land because he went for a flight and never came back. He always got to explore first. He'd be there when we arrived, and greet us with a bored look on his face, as though he had seen everything already and was anxious to go somewhere else.

I had debated entering Australia secretly, and keeping the sub hidden, as we were used to doing, but had decided against it. Ever since I first went to sea I had been an outlaw, because registering the sub required an inspection, and the Canadian government had a zillion rules and regulations, and the chances of getting a homemade submarine registered were next to none. So, I just went to sea without papers. And that made me an outlaw.

But two officers from the South African navy kindly registered the sub in Port Elizabeth, South Africa, returning a favour for a friend of theirs I had helped. That made the sub legal for the very first time, and me no longer an outlaw. While I didn't know if that would hold up in Canada, it ought to work everywhere else. Still, I was nervous calling the harbour authorities in Perth to request permission to moor. What if they decided the sub was a threat to the security of Australia, or judged it unseaworthy? By the Law of the Sea they had the right to seize it. They probably wouldn't, but they *could*, and that made me nervous.

I called the harbour authorities on the shortwave when we entered the twelve-mile territorial zone of Australia. I wasn't actually sure if we had entered it or not—it wasn't like there was a sign floating in the water that said "Twelve-Mile Zone"—I just guessed. It took awhile to explain who I was, and what my vessel was. Harbour police never expect to see a civilian submarine. If you say, "submarine," they always assume it is a military sub, and their voices get really stiff over the radio.

But the Customs officers who came out to meet us two miles off shore were very friendly. There were three of them in an outboard harbour boat: two men and one woman. They were carrying machine guns, which was what I had expected. Canadian officials did the same. Over the radio I was ordered to stay on the surface all the way in, and leave the hatch open, which I did. I was also told to have the entire crew on deck when the harbour boat rendezvoused with us, which I did, holding Hollie in my arms. Seaweed was already gone. He didn't take orders from anybody but himself.

They approached quickly, and circled us three times before cutting their engines and coasting to a stop. Once they had a good look at Hollie and me, they were all smiles. "G'day!" they yelled through a megaphone. "Welcome to Australia!"

They inspected the sub in ten minutes, asked me a few questions, stamped my passport, and offered us a berth in Jervoise Bay, about six miles south of Fremantle, Perth's enormous harbour. I happily accepted. We followed them in at eight knots, and they showed us where to tie up. Then they wished us good luck, waved, and sped away. I had heard that Australians were friendly. In all our travels, I had never felt so welcome as I did here. And how wonderful it was to come in legally.

The berth was in a small floating pier, with enough room for about a dozen boats. I tied up on the berth furthest from shore. Only three boats were moored, and there was no one around. It was too shallow to submerge, but I let enough water into the tanks to sink the hull just beneath the surface, until we were more or less sitting on the bottom. Only the portal was showing now, sticking up two feet above the pier, like an industrial drain. When the tide came in, the sub would rise with it, and the portal would maintain roughly the same position. You would only know there was a submarine there if you walked out onto the pier and stared into the water.

At first, I figured they gave us this spot because it was far from the fancy, crowded marinas of Fremantle Harbour, where a submarine would draw unwanted attention. But a quick glance in the other direction revealed another reason— we were moored next to a naval dockyard. Perhaps they wanted the navy to keep an eye on us. On the other side of the navy was an oil refinery. Everywhere else I looked I saw industry. We were in the industrial zone, not the prettiest corner of the city, but I was more than grateful to have the berth.

I grabbed my hat, sunscreen, money, water, and dog biscuits. I emptied the tool bag, wiped it clean, and put Hollie inside. It was the perfect size for a small dog, and he could lie down and sleep whenever he got tired of walking. It had a wooden frame with nylon mesh sides, and was comfortable on my back. I climbed out of the portal, shut the hatch, and sealed it. If we were going to start mooring in public places, maybe it was time to get a lock.

Standing on the little pier, I took one final look at the sub. It seemed so tiny here, next to the other boats, tied up like a mule. I could hardly believe we had just crossed an ocean with it. I was taught that you cannot love an inanimate object, you can only love a person, or maybe an animal. Well, I guess I was breaking that rule, because I loved my submarine.

I crossed the pier, bent down, and let Hollie out of the tool bag. He stood for a second or two, just staring at me, trembling, waiting for me to say it was okay. "It's okay, Hollie. You can go."

He ran up the sandy bank to the road, shaking with excitement, and I followed him. The sand felt strange beneath my feet, as it always did after being at sea for a long time. But the strangeness lasted only about ten minutes. Then it felt as though we had never left the land. There were palm trees and dry deciduous trees lining the road. It looked like a cross between Africa and Canada. Hollie looked up at me. His eyes were wet with excitement. "We're in Australia, Hollie! *Australia! Woo Hoo!*"

We walked for three hours, which went by like nothing because we were so thrilled to be walking we hardly noticed the heat, until I realized that my mouth was so dry I almost couldn't swallow. It was hot! Hollie was smart, though. He knew how to walk in my shadow when the sun was strong. When we turned ninety degrees onto a new street, and my shadow shifted, he'd find it and stay in it. Sometimes he'd walk beside me, or behind me, or in front of me, but always in my shadow. Whenever I stopped for a drink of water, I'd give him one, too. We had taken long walks in the Pacific, India, South Africa—all hot places—but I'd have to say that the sun in Australia *felt* hotter. And that's what my guidebook said, too. A page with stern warnings about the dangers of the sun was titled: "Mad Dogs and Englishmen Go Out in the Midday Sun."

But it was a strange kind of dryness. In Canada, we'd say that these trees were dead. Here, they seemed to be doing all right. Whenever they were close to a source of water, they were green. Whenever they weren't, they were yellow, brown, or grey, but still had leaves clinging to them. The soil beneath them was sandy, slightly red, and dry as dust. I could sense the outback not far away, and beyond it, the desert, where the origins of the rivers that emptied into the harbour narrowed to dry riverbeds, where the pipes of the city's water system didn't reach, and trees didn't grow. I was keen to see all of that, but not on this first walk, of course. For now I was just happy we could stretch our legs for a few hours.

After the first three hours, Hollie was resting in the tool bag, panting like a little motor on my back, and I was walking in the shade as much as I possibly could. By the late afternoon we had reached the centre of town, where I found something I was anxiously seeking—a real Italian pizzeria. It looked like a little piece of Italy in Australia, although it was air-conditioned inside, and that made it feel as though we had walked into the Arctic. I chose a booth by the window, let Hollie out of the tool bag, and peeled the sweaty t-shirt away from my back. Hollie sat so quietly beside me no one noticed him. And when the waitress came, she just smiled at him. I ordered a large pizza, two tall glasses of pop, a special plate of toppings for Hollie, and a large bowl of water. It was hard to wait because we were so hungry. Then, when our meal finally came, and I took my first bite, I immediately thought of Margaret. It bothered me that I had never thought to ask her whether she had enough food. Why didn't I do that? Then I couldn't help smiling a little, because I knew she wouldn't approve of me worrying about her at all. Not one little bit.

Before I finished eating, I heard noises outside. Hollie was flat on his side now in deep sleep, and didn't hear anything. Outside, a parade was going by. I waited until it passed by the window, then stood up and watched. Hundreds of people were marching up the street, carrying poles with slogans on them. It wasn't a parade; it was a protest. I had never seen a real protest before, so I paid for our meal, put the rest of the pizza into a box, slid Hollie into the tool bag, and went out to follow the marchers.

They went up one street and down another, shouting, "NO MORE MINING! SAVE OUR PLANET! NO MORE MINING! SAVE OUR PLANET!" It was an environmental protest! I had surely come to the right place.

The protestors marched to the front of a large government building, and stopped. There were police on horseback there, but they didn't look surprised or angry. The protestors didn't look angry either. Everything was well organized and orderly, as if it were something they did every week. A handful of protestors took turns speaking from a megaphone. They had strong Australian accents, and it was a little hard for me to understand. Mostly they seemed to be demanding that the government stop giving tax breaks to mining companies, and put more money into saving the environment. They wanted big oil companies to pay for their oil spills, and they wanted more money spent on saving whales, sharks, and turtles. I couldn't have agreed more. Then I heard one person say to another, "Ahh, they just say the same things. They never change anything." "Yeah, but just wait till Brass-knuckles Bennett has a turn," said another. "They'll get an earful then." "Who's Brass-knuckles Bennett?" asked the first. "A big-shot barrister from Sydney. Goes to bat for the whales."

I moved closer as a large man stepped up to a podium and took hold of a microphone. TV cameras closed in on him as he spoke. I strained to hear every word.

He was a big man but had a soft voice. There was something very compelling about it, so that I think I would have listened carefully even if he were selling farm machinery. He looked like someone who might sell farm machinery, too, not practise law. Basically, he said the same things that Margaret had said: that too much damage had been done to the environment already, and that it was too late to stop global warming. All we can do now, he said, is buy time and try to save the things we can, but we can only buy time if we stop opening new coal mines and refineries, and close down the old ones. If we don't do that, and do it now, he said, then we can kiss the Earth goodbye sooner rather than later.

It was the same message Margaret had given me, and yet, somehow, with his gentle manner and soft voice, it hit home even harder for me. I felt as though I was listening to a soft-spoken angel declaring the end of the world.

When the protest was over, I wandered back to the industrial pier with a heavy heart. Was it really too late? If so, why did the world still look okay to me? I mean, I had been all around it, and had seen some terrible things, yet never got the impression it was actually dying. I knew it was in trouble, not dying. Still, that speaker's words affected me deeply. They were so measured and certain I almost felt the air had less oxygen in it than it had before he spoke.

Chapter Eight

SHE WAS SITTING ON THE floating pier beside the sub. She was the only one there. I was pretty sure I had seen her at the demonstration. I wondered what she was doing here.

She was about thirty years old, I was guessing; it was hard for me to gauge the age of anyone over twenty. Her hair was light brown, her eyes blue, and her face had a soft expression, as if she were an animal caretaker, or kindergarten teacher, or something like that. She was about my height, and athletic, but not a sailor. I could tell by the way she was staring at the sea. She wasn't looking at the sub, either, even though she was sitting right beside it, and could see it easily enough, and that gave me the impression she wasn't interested in it. She fooled me that way.

"Hi," I said, because she pretended she didn't see me when I stepped onto the pier. Hollie followed at my feet.

"G'day," she said. "You're going to sea, are ya?" She had that kind of Australian accent that made every sentence sound playful.

"Yes. Eventually."

"Is the little dog going with ya?"

"Yes."

"That's all right. Where are you going to next?"

I looked at her. There was something behind her questions, I could feel it, but didn't know what it was. "We're going to Tasmania. We've got a few weeks of sailing ahead of us first."

"That's all right, too. That's quite the contraption you've got there. Been at sea long?"

"A couple of years."

"How old are ya?"

"Sixteen. Turning seventeen."

She almost laughed, but caught herself. I figured she was going to keep asking me questions unless I asked her one. So I did. "Did I see you at the protest today?"

She smiled. "Yeah. Ya did."

"You must be interested in saving the environment then."

"Yeah, I sure am. And you?"

"That's why I'm here. I want to learn how to save the oceans."

"That's brilliant. Good on you. Did you learn anything at the protest today?"

"I think so. I learned something from listening to that big lawyer."

"A lawyer?" Now she was really curious. "Who was that then?"

"I don't know his real name, but I heard somebody call him 'Brass-knuckles Bennett.'"

She laughed, dropped her head, and shook it from side to side. "Brass-knuckles Bennett?"

"Do you know who he is?"

"Yah, I know who that is."

"You do?"

"Yeah. That's me."

"What?" She must have been joking. "But ... he was a man."

"Yeah, that was Pritchard Lovelace you were listening to. He's a good speaker."

"Sorry."

"No worries. I get that a lot. When people hear you're a tough barrister, they just assume you're a man. Anyone called 'Brass-knuckles Bennett' must be a man, right?" She stuck out her hand. "My name's Jewels. What's yours?"

"Alfred." We shook hands. "Why do they call you 'Brass-knuckles Bennett?"

"Well, Bennett's my last name, by marriage. The brass-knuckles part comes from the fact that I don't like to lose. So I fight hard."

"Hate to lose what?"

"In court. And, usually, I don't. But today I did. And the

thing that I lost to is sitting right over there." She pointed south.

"The navy? You lost to the navy?"

She shook her head. "Look a little beyond that."

"There's just the oil refinery."

"Right."

"You lost to the oil refinery?"

"Not exactly. Have you got a pair of binoculars in your submarine by any chance?"

"Yes, I do."

"Can we have a look? Would you mind?"

"Not at all. Just a second." I opened the hatch, climbed in with Hollie, and put him down. He went straight to his water dish, I climbed back out with the binoculars. "Here they are," I said, and passed them to her.

She raised them and looked. "Yeah. There it is. The *Indigo*. Have a look." She handed the binoculars back.

"What is it?"

"A tanker."

"Oh." I took a look. "I see her."

"Yeah, why do you sailors always call a ship a *her*? What's that about?"

"I don't know; it's a tradition."

"That's a steel machine weighing who knows how many thousands of tons, and its belly is filling up with stinky black oil, and you call it a 'her' as if she's a little girl or something."

I stared at Jewels. I wondered what she wanted. I could tell she wanted something.

"Tell me, Alfred. Can you make tea on your submarine?"

"Yes, I can. Would you like some?"

"I would wrestle a croc for a cup of tea."

"Come in."

So she followed me in. She came down the ladder slowly, and found a spot on the floor beside the observation window in the bow, next to Hollie's blanket. It was the only comfortable spot I had for a guest. I brought her a pillow to sit on, then put a pot of water on for tea. Jewels looked around curiously, but wasn't as interested in the sub as people usually were. I didn't think she was much impressed by machines.

"So, where are you from, Alfred? And what brings you to Australia?" I passed her a cup of tea, and she raised the cup to her lips, took a sip carefully, and stared at me. She was studying me. I felt as though I was on the witness stand.

"I'm from Newfoundland, Canada, and I've been sailing around the world for almost a year now, but I've been at sea on and off for two and a half years. I came here because I want to become an active environmentalist, if it's not too late, and I heard that Australia is the best place to learn about it."

She smiled with genuine enthusiasm. "This is synchronistic, Alfred."

"What does that mean?"

"It means that we were meant to meet, because I'm keen to save the environment, too. But tell me, why did you say, 'if it's not too late?' What's that about?"

"Well, I met somebody at sea who told me that it's definitely too late. And that speaker at the protest said it is. And scientists on the radio say it is. Do you think it *isn't*?"

"Are you alive?"

"Yes."

"Then it's not too late." Jewels took another sip of tea, and stared over the cup at me. She was thinking of something else for sure. I wondered when she'd come out with it. "You're from Canada, you're a sailor, and you want to become an environmentalist, so . . . you must know about the Sea Shepherd Society, right?"

"I think I've heard of them, but I don't know who they are."

"You don't?"

"No."

"And Captain Paul Watson? You know who he is, right? He's a Canadian hero."

"No."

She laughed. "You're a wannabe environmentalist from Canada and you've never heard of one of the most important environmentalists in the world, who's from your own country?"

"No. Who is he?"

"He's the patron saint of whales. He created the Sea Shepherd Society to stop the slaughter of whales, dolphins, and other creatures in the sea. But he's not your typical environmentalist. He's more like a vigilante. He's a whaler's worst nightmare. He flies the Jolly Roger."

"The skull and crossbones? Is he a pirate?"

"He is if you're killing whales. Otherwise, he's a pretty nice guy. Right now, he's in Hobart, getting ready to return to the Southern Ocean to fight Japanese whalers who are not supposed to be there, but who go there every year to hunt whales anyway. You must know that there's a moratorium on whaling, right?"

"Yes."

"Well, the waters of the Southern Ocean constitute a special whale sanctuary. They're protected waters. Nobody's allowed to hunt there. And yet, Japanese whalers hunt and kill thousands of whales every year, and call it 'research.' Then they sell the meat on the market. Everyone knows it's not for research, but nobody has the guts to stop them, except Captain Watson. Nobody lives in Antarctica, so there's no police force, which is why the Sea Shepherd Society must go there, find the whalers, and stop them. They do everything they can to prevent the killing. If you want to be an environmentalist, Alfred, then you must agree with them, right?"

"Yes, of course."

"And that's why I'm here from Sydney. That tanker over there, the *Indigo*, is filling up with oil as we speak. The day after tomorrow, *she's* scheduled to sail for the Southern Ocean, where *she's* not supposed go, because oil tankers are not permitted below the 60-degree latitude line, where an oil spill would be catastrophic for whales, seals, penguins, and all sea life. But no one's stopping her. That tanker is going to refuel the whalers so that they can keep hunting. Otherwise, they'd have to go home. So that's why I'm here, to bring a court injunction to stop the *Indigo* from leaving port tomorrow."

"But it didn't work?"

"That's right, because the pockets of oil companies are deeper than everybody else's, and politicians are in the habit of rewarding whoever funds their political campaigns. So, we lost this battle, but not the war. Did you follow that?"

"I think so."

Jewels took another sip of tea, and stared over the cup. "Alfred?"

Here it comes. "Yes?"

"Let me ask you a hypothetical question."

"Okay."

"Let's say you wanted to stop a ship like the *Indigo* from leaving port, just for a week or so. What would you do, short of blowing it up? I'm just talking hypothetically here, of course. I'm not being serious."

She sure sounded serious. "What would *I* do?"

"Yeah, what would *you* do, but so that you wouldn't get caught? Just for fun, what would you do?"

I thought about it. "Well, I might try wrapping ropes around the propeller. They'd twist up and shut the engine down maybe, and possibly cause some engine damage. Well, it would burn out the engine of a smaller boat for sure, but maybe not a tanker. The big engines of a tanker probably have safety features built in to protect them from things like that. Probably it would shut them down just for a day or so."

"But for longer than that, what would you do? Just hypothetically."

She stared at me so closely it felt as though she were counting the hairs of my eyelashes. I stared back. She didn't look like the kind of person who would sabotage a tanker. On the other hand, I didn't know what a person like that looked like. "I suppose if I really had to stop a ship from leaving port, I'd probably cut through the blades of the propeller with a blow torch, or at least part way. Then, I'd wrap a chain around the blades underwater, so that when the ship started up her engines, the chain would snap the propeller blades clear off. The propeller of a tanker like that has probably got four blades, or maybe five. You'd probably have to cut through just two blades to keep her from sailing. I'm guessing it would take them at least a couple of weeks to get another propeller, if not a month. I think that's what I'd do. I sure wouldn't want to get caught though."

"No, of course not. It's just a hypothetical question anyway. Nobody's going to do that." She smiled strangely. "How long would it take to cut through two blades?"

"Probably a couple of hours. Maybe more. But it would have to be somebody who knows how to operate a welding torch under water. That's a pretty specialized skill. And you'd have to do it right next to the navy. That'd be pretty crazy."

"I suppose."

"And that's sabotage."

"Yeah."

"Maybe it's terrorism."

"Nah, that's not terrorism." Jewels sipped her tea and stared at the periscope, but her eyes were out of focus. Her mind was far away. I might have guessed where.

Chapter Nine

WE WERE UP BEFORE the sun. I took three water bottles, a bag of dog biscuits, my jacket, hat, sunscreen, sleeping mat, one-man tent, two hundred dollars, and squeezed it all into a knapsack. The knapsack hung over one shoulder, and the tool bag hung over the other, criss-crossing my front. I climbed out with Hollie, put him down on the bank with all of the stuff, and told him to wait there. He didn't like that, but he obeyed me. Then I went back to the sub.

I motored out to the small breakwater that protected the pier. It was just a hundred feet away, but the harbour floor dropped to seventy-five feet there. I wanted to set the sub on the bottom, out of sight, and out of temptation. By the Law of the Sea, a foreign submarine had to stay on the surface inside a country's three-mile zone. I knew that. But I wasn't actually leaving the area of the pier I was just submerging within it. I planned to take a longer hike with Hollie, because I wanted to see a little of Australia before we went back to sea, and I wasn't comfortable leaving the sub where people could climb in and steal stuff, or fiddle around with the controls, or even start the engine and head out to sea. Any sub could become incredibly dangerous in the wrong hands. I figured the harbour police would agree with that, and would understand me wanting to hide it because they were the ones who gave me the isolated berth in the first place.

But setting the sub on the bottom was not my favourite thing to do, because it meant I had to open the hatch under water, climb out, shut the hatch, seal it, and swim to the surface. I had done it a number of times before, but it was always unnerving. If I could be as fast as the last time, only a couple of feet of water would enter the sub, and the sump pumps would remove that in less than ten minutes. If something went wrong, and the sub completely flooded, it would probably take an hour for the pumps to empty it. There wasn't much danger to me climbing out, unless I slipped, fell, and banged my head. But I knew that wouldn't happen. I was so comfortable under water. I could hold my breath for two minutes when I was calm, and that was plenty of time to seal the hatch and swim to the surface. Climbing *into* the sub was much harder.

And so, I descended to the bottom and shut everything off, except for the pale blue emergency light that used very little power but let me make my way around inside. I picked up everything off the floor and put it on my bed. I did a double check to make sure the compartments in the stern were sealed, then climbed the ladder, took a few deep breaths, and spun the wheel. I waited until it was completely unsealed before pushing the hatch up and letting the sea flood into the sub. No matter how many times I did this, it was always a shock. On the outside, I was calm, and my movements were quick, careful, and measured. Inside, I always had to fight down a feeling of panic. I pulled myself out against the incredible force of water trying to push me back down. It was so strong! I felt like a rat crawling out of a flooding sewer drain. But once I was out, shutting the hatch was easy. I spun the wheel from the outside, sealed it, and swam to the surface. When I stuck my head out of the water, I saw a yellowish orange streak in the east. The sun had travelled across the desert, and was about to reach the sea. It was time for a seriously long walk.

Hollie greeted me excitedly when I stepped from the water, and, for the first time since arriving in Perth, so did Seaweed. I was so glad to see him because we were walking away from the coast now, and he wouldn't be able to spot the sub, and would wonder where we were. Maybe he would think we had left without him. I knew that Seaweed would always survive wherever he was, because he was tough and resourceful, but I sure didn't want to lose him.

We walked to the mouth of Fremantle Harbour once again, and then followed it inland until it became the Swan River. It was dark when we started out, but by the time we reached the point at which the harbour became a river, it was late morning. After being cooped up in a submarine for a whole month, it wasn't hard to walk all day. And that's what I intended to do for several more days.

It was especially nice once we were walking beside the river, because the river was beautiful, and lined with trees and parks, and we often had shade to walk in, and rest in, and later to sleep in. We also had access to shops for the first day, which weren't too far from the river, and pizza, and another of the pleasures I missed at sea—candy. I stuffed my pockets with it, and ate it pretty much constantly on the first day. Then I had to buy a toothbrush and toothpaste, because I had forgotten to bring mine along, and my teeth had grown a thick layer of plaque on them. I didn't give Hollie or Seaweed any candy because it wasn't good for them, but I did share a bag of popcorn.

The river narrowed surprisingly quickly as we travelled upstream beside it. By the end of the first day, we were standing on the bank of a gently flowing current that I could easily have swum across with one breath. It was hard to believe we were just miles away from where the river turned into one of the world's greatest harbours.

In one of the last shops along the way, I was able to buy a frozen pizza. I carried it for a few hours to let it thaw, and the three of us sat on the riverbank and ate it raw beneath the shade of a humongous tree, with hundreds of snake-like roots that spread around us like a basket. Cooked pizza was a lot better. Still, we were happy to have it.

The soil of the riverbank where we sat was dry, spongy, and soft, and I figured it was a good place to sleep. We were outside of the city now. There were a few scattered houses, very few shops, and some farms. The whole area was incredibly beautiful, although unbelievably dry. In Canada, we'd call this a drought. In fact, Australia looked like what Canada might look like if we had a drought that lasted for a hundred years.

Under the branches of the tree I rolled out my mat and pulled my jacket over myself like a blanket. Hollie made himself cosy on the ground beside me. Seaweed sat by my feet, facing the river. I felt safe having the nose and ears of a dog, and the eyes of a seagull, to watch for spiders and snakes at night. Australia had a *lot* of poisonous spiders and snakes. As we drifted to sleep, we could hear ripples in the river, but mostly it was silent. Looking beyond the treetops, I watched the stars blink silently, and thought what a wonderful life we had. But I couldn't watch for long because the weight of sleep fell heavily upon me.

Waking from one of the best sleeps of my life, I stood up and stretched as the crew stretched. I rolled up the sleeping mat, packed up our things, and headed off to find a grocery store. It wasn't easy to find one now, and we had to walk quite a ways from the river before we spotted a small store that was attached to a house. Stepping inside, I found that it took my eyes awhile to adjust to the darkness. The first thing I spied were bags of candy, which I couldn't resist. I also bought a jar of peanut butter, a jar of jam, a loaf of bread, a bag of granola, four oranges, four bananas, a bottle of milk, and a jug of water. I had to carry the water jug in my hands, but it had a handle that made that easier, and I could switch hands. We couldn't go into a dry nature reserve without water, and I didn't know if the water in the river was safe to drink.

As I stood at the cash with Hollie at my feet, waiting for the clerk to ring in our groceries, I looked up at the TV screen above his head, which was showing the news. There was a picture of a ship down at the harbour—a tanker. Then there was a picture of a really large propeller under water, with two blades missing! I froze! The sound on the TV was low, and it was too difficult to make out what the news people were saying, but they showed a sketch of a small submarine, a sketch of a young man, and a small dog. My head started to spin, and I felt sick to my stomach. I wanted to ask the man at the counter to turn up the volume but didn't want to draw attention to us. I paid for our groceries, thanked the man, and went out the door. My heart was thumping in my chest.

Outside, I stared at the telephone booth. Maybe I could call them and tell them that it wasn't me, and that the sub is still there at the bottom of the pier. I could explain how we had walked all day yesterday, and slept by the river, and couldn't possibly have sabotaged the tanker. That was a good idea. I stepped inside the booth and reached for the phone book. Then I hesitated. If I called them, and told them it wasn't me, they'd ask me if I knew who it was, and I'd have to tell them I didn't know, because there was no way I would tell on Jewels. Problem was, I wasn't very good at lying, especially under pressure. And they would most certainly put me under pressure if they brought me in for questioning. And if they did bring me in—which they would surely do—and kept me locked up for a month or two while they figured it all out, what would become of Hollie and Seaweed?

I stepped out of the phone booth and walked slowly back to the river. I needed to think it through. Someone had sabotaged the tanker, and had been put up to it by Jewels, who had received the idea from me. Did that make me responsible? Or was it possible that somebody else had come up with the same idea? That seemed unlikely, though I supposed it was possible. Either way, they thought it had been me. And they would come looking for me now. And I doubted they'd bother to search the bottom of the pier. They'd think we had sailed away. They'd search for us at sea.

Chapter Ten

WE FOLLOWED THE RIVER into Walyunga National Park, which was filled with trees, rocks, hills, and gorges, and, with its dry red earth, was what I imagined Mars might look like if it had trees. The walk along the river was well shaded, secluded, and wonderful, even though I was nervous in my gut all day. But I had come up with a plan.

Since the police, coast guard, and navy would be searching for us at sea, and would assume we were trying to sail away; then, after a week or so, when they hadn't found us, they'd surely think we were gone for good, and would stop searching. So all we had to do was stay away from the pier for about a week or so, sneak in at night, motor the sub under another ship, and follow it out to sea. We'd appear as one vessel on sonar, and be undetectable by radar. Then, once we were out of Australian waters, I would contact the Perth harbour police on shortwave, and explain exactly what had happened—that it hadn't been me, and that I didn't know who it was.

I thought it was a good plan, and it might have worked, except for one very unlucky moment. Just before entering the park, I went searching for a small store to buy more water and snacks. We were eating and drinking more food and water than on the sub. If we were going to disappear into the woods for a week, we had to have more of both. But the only store I could find was inside a small garage, and didn't offer much. I went in without taking my hat off, and left Hollie outside in the tool bag, in the shade. I felt confident no one would recognize me from the picture that had been on the news, especially when it didn't even look like me.

There was a gruff looking man sitting behind the counter eating a bowl of soup out of a Styrofoam bowl when I came in. He looked up when he saw me, and said, "G'day."

"G'day!" I said, trying to sound Australian. I picked up a jug of water, a bottle of milk, five bags of nacho chips, three bags of trail mix, a box of cookies, a handful of chocolate bars, and a large bag of peppermints. You needed lots of sugar when you were walking all day. As I put the things down on the counter, beside a pile of newspapers, I saw the story of the tanker sabotage on the very first page, including the sketch of

Hollie and me. I pretended to ignore it. That's when another man came inside the store, carrying Hollie in the tool bag.

"Is this your dog?" he said.

I turned and looked at him. He seemed kind, the sort of person who loves animals.

"Yes," I said. "He's mine."

"I heard something whining outside and couldn't figure out where it was coming from. Then I saw him in the bag. You didn't have to leave him outside, mate. We let dogs in the store. He's a cute little fellah, isn't he?"

"Yes, he is." I turned around to pay for my things, but now the man behind the counter was staring at Hollie. Then he stared at me. And then he stared at the newspaper. He didn't say a word, but his eyes were a little wider than before. I paid for our stuff, thanked both men, and left the garage, but I could feel their eyes on my back as we walked away.

Had he recognized us? I was pretty sure that he had. When we reached the park, we disappeared into the woods, and spent the rest of the day hiking up and down the hills, heading east. But I couldn't stop worrying about the man in the garage. Would he report us to the police? I had to assume that he would.

That night, I heard the engine of a jeep roaming through the park as we slept in our tent. Was it police, or was it just park officials on regular patrol? I had pitched the tent beneath the boughs of a tree in the most secluded spot I could find. I wanted to stay inside to guard against snakes and spiders, and Hollie stayed with me. Seaweed slept on the roof, but kept sliding off noisily and waking us up. At one point, the engine sounded very near, and I lay still, wondering if they had found us. Then the sound went away, but I couldn't tell if that was because they had turned the engine off, or had just disappeared over a hill. Suddenly, I heard what I thought were boots on the ground. I sat up. They were coming so fast. How could they have found us in the middle of the night? They couldn't have spotted us from the air. And we hadn't lit a fire, or used any light. It didn't make sense. How could they have found us?

They were coming so quickly I didn't see how we could run for it. Running through the woods at night was difficult, especially when it was hilly. How was it *they* were able to move so quickly? I couldn't figure it out. And yet, they didn't come directly to where we were. They circled us a few times. Were they just guessing? I was surprised at how much noise they were making. Suddenly it occurred to me that they weren't police officers at all, because I heard Hollie make his little growl, and he only growled at animals.

I opened the zipper of the tent and poked my head outside. There, under the light of the moon, I watched a herd of shadows race through the trees, pounding the spongy earth as they went. I couldn't see them clearly, but I knew now what they were. Kangaroos. Amazing. They were as fast as deer.

The next day, we started walking as soon as there was light. We continued east, judging by the sun, and walked where the trees were thickest. But it was unnerving. Several times we had to duck down when we were close to a trail or road, and a jeep came by. What I was really afraid of was that they would come looking for us with dogs. We'd never have a chance of escaping them then. But I wasn't even certain they were looking for us.

We saw more kangaroos in the early morning, and again in the twilight. Once again, they reminded me of deer, because they seemed very gentle. They were nocturnal, too, as were wombats, which we also saw, shuffling along the ground like miniature tanks, and pushing everything out of their way. Hollie growled at them ever so quietly, but they completely ignored him. The wildlife of Australia was so different from the wildlife of Canada it was hard to believe. This was especially true with the birds. As twilight settled in a valley we were passing through, we heard what sounded like a chorus of insane circus clowns laughing their heads off. The sound echoed all around us as if it were coming from speakers on every tree. I was completely bewildered at first, but then remembered having heard the sound before on TV, and knew what it was: the kookaburra—a small bird with an unbelievably big call. It was hauntingly funny. In Canada, we had the mournful song of the loon, the cry of the coyote, and the howl of the wolf, but I doubted there was any sound in Canada that could match the crazy hysterical wailing of the kookaburra.

By the end of the second day, we had walked out of Walyunga National Park and into Avon National Park, and the Swan River had become the Avon River. Following the river like a shadow were train tracks, and I would have liked to walk on them, but they were too exposed to the air. So we stayed in the trees, but usually within sight of both the tracks and the river. The river was just a stream now, easy to step over, but also too exposed to travel on. It was a lot of work climbing up and down the hills, and by the time we crawled into the tent, we were exhausted. I slept without waking, and if kangaroos, or anything else, had come by, I never heard them. By the morning, just when I was starting to think that we were not being chased at all, we were discovered.

We had slept in. Walking for a few days in the heat of Australia took more out of us than I would have guessed. I didn't wake when I normally would have, nor did Hollie, and Seaweed didn't care if we were up or not. I had pitched the tent on top of a hill in a group of trees. You couldn't see it from the road, or the river, or train tracks, but you could see it from the air. The sun must have been up for two or three hours when I heard the buzz of a small airplane in the distance.

"Hollie! Quick!" I jumped up, unzipped the front of the tent, and scooted Hollie out. Then I pulled down the poles, gathered the tent together as quickly as I could, and shoved it into the knapsack. But I think we were too late. To us, the plane looked far away, but I knew from experience that when you're searching for something with binoculars, you'll see it long before it will see you. Even so, I stood still against the trunk of the tree and held Hollie in my arms as the plane passed overhead. It made a few close passes before it went away. If there were jeeps in the area in communication with the plane, we were in trouble.

I just didn't want to get caught. In a way, things weren't as bad as they might have been because I hadn't actually done anything wrong. And I could sort of prove it. The fact that we had been walking for a few days, and could find witnesses in stores to verify that; and the fact that the sub was still on the harbour floor, ought to convince the police that we had nothing to do with the sabotage. But I didn't want them to hold me against my will and separate me from my crew. And I didn't want to get Jewels into trouble. What if they made me take a lie-detector test, and I failed it?

But those weren't the only reasons I didn't want to get caught. Knowing that somebody was chasing me made me feverishly determined to get away. Maybe I was crazy, but I wanted to know that I could escape if I really had to. At sea, I always could. Maybe if I put my mind to it, I could here, too.

And so, I changed tactics. Instead of keeping to the woods, I went down to the river and started jogging downstream. We were heading back towards the city now, at least for a while. There were lots of large rocks in the river, especially where it was dry, and if the plane came back, I planned to hide in the shadow of one. I could also curl up in a ball in the stream itself, stay absolutely still and pretend to be a rock. Travelling through the river would also allow us to escape if they brought dogs out, because the dogs would lose our scent in the water.

For a while it seemed to work. I heard the plane two more times, but it was distant. Then, I heard a train coming. For a moment I got excited, because I thought maybe we could hop onto it, and catch a ride all the way back into the city. But the instant I saw it, I knew that was impossible. It was moving way too fast. It would have been suicide.

But the noise of the train was a disaster, because it lasted a long time, and prevented me from hearing the sound of two jeeps that were coming closer all the time. By the time I heard them they could see me.

They were on a hill a couple of hundred feet from the river. It was too late to hide in the river now. Instead, I jumped out, ran up the bank, through the trees, and down the hill. As I went over the crest of the hill, I heard their engines rev higher. The chase was on.

The road didn't follow the river closely at that point, because of the hills, which was a big help to me. In my mind, I was preparing what I would say if they caught me. I'd pretend I didn't know what they were talking about, and say that I was only running because they were chasing me, and that I didn't know why they were.

At the bottom of the hill I stopped and listened for the jeeps. At first, I heard nothing. But then there was a distant whirring sound that could only have been their engines whining as they raced around the winding dirt road. Instead of running further down the hill, to where they would eventually catch up with me, I did the opposite; I ran back up to where we had been. It was kind of steep, and a lot of work for Hollie. When we reached the top, I lifted him up and put him in the tool bag. He was ready for a rest now but I was bursting with energy.

Back up the hill, I crossed the river and ran to the next rise. I wanted to cross the road and reach the highest point on the hill, and from there, decide which way to go. The road snaked around the hill in sharp turns that made it difficult to identify where sounds were coming from, and that led me to make a second mistake. I heard what I took to be the distant sound of jeeps' engines way down the hill. Instead, it turned out to be the engine of a third jeep just around the corner. I scrambled across the road and tried to get into the bushes before it saw me, but was too late. As I jumped across the bank, the jeep skidded to a stop on the road, spraying dust and small rocks everywhere. I lay still where I landed, holding the tool bag in my arms, and trying to breathe quietly. I heard a door open and someone jump out. Shoot! I dropped my head. How I hated to get caught. Maybe I could still make a run for it by going up the hill. They'd have to chase me on foot, and maybe they wouldn't catch me. Surely they wouldn't shoot at me, or, if they did, they'd warn me first and I would stop. I got ready to bolt when I heard someone call my name. "Alfred!" He didn't yell it though; he whispered it. I raised my head out of the bush. I saw a young man in shorts and t-shirt.

He waved his arm frantically at me. "Hurry up, mate! Come with me. I'm Brian Bennett."

I stared at him, trying to figure out what was going on. I had no idea who he was.

"I'm Jewels' husband. Jump in! I'm going to get you out of here. Hurry up, mate, they're coming for you!"

I jumped out of the bush and scrambled onto the road. He reached around and opened the back door. "Quick, jump in and hide under the seat! Pull that blanket over you!"

I did as I was told. I climbed in with Hollie, lay down on the floor of the jeep, squeezed under the seat as well as I could, and pulled the blanket over us. There wasn't much room. He shut the door, spun around on the road, and went back the way he had come. It was a bumpy ride, but I was happy we were escaping. My only concern now was for Seaweed. What would he do when he couldn't find us?

Chapter Eleven

"IT WASN'T JEWELS. I don't know who it was, mate, but it wasn't Jewels. She'd never do such a thing."

Brian was speaking loudly over the noise of the engine, road, and wind through the open windows, and I had to yell back. It was an old jeep, and there was no air-conditioning. The engine whined and hissed up and down the hills in the dry heat. The road wasn't so bumpy now, but every time he made a sharp turn, I had to grab the underbelly of the seat, and hold onto Hollie. I couldn't see anything either, which made me very uncomfortable.

"You don't sound Australian," I said.

"Aye, that'd be 'cause I'm not."

"Where are you from?"

"Ireland, my son. Didn't she tell you that?"

"No. We didn't talk that long, really."

"Lots of Irish folk down here. You're from Canada, are you?"

"Yes. Newfoundland."

"Any good fishin' there?"

"Yah, pretty good."

"I'll have to go an' see it for myself then." Brian turned the steering wheel sharply, and we left the road and went over a steep hill. He drove fast, as if we were in a cross-country race. I wondered if anyone could hear us shouting. "Have you found yourself in situations like this before, Alfred?"

"Not exactly like this. Usually it's at sea."

"That's right, you're travelling the world in a submarine. But where is it then? Where do you leave a submarine when you're not using it?"

I realized I had to make a decision about whether I could really trust Brian or not. Probably I could, but I wasn't certain.

"What is Jewels' nickname?"

"My wife?" He laughed. "Aye, that'd be Brass-knuckles Bennett. You don't trust me then. Can't say I blame you. You've got good reasons to be suspicious."

He could have known those things. "What was the name of the man I thought was her?" He could only know that if she told him, and I figured she would have told her husband that.

"Ahh . . . that'd be that Lovelace fellah. Richard . . . is that his name? Big fella with a soft voice. Doesn't look anything like my wife." He laughed again.

"Yah, that's him. My sub's sitting on the harbour floor."

"On the bottom?"

"Yah."

"Right there in the harbour?"

"Yup."

"Right next to the navy?"

"Yup."

He burst out laughing. "And they're out looking for you all over kingdom come, and your submarine's sitting right there under their noses." He paused. "Why didn't you just tell them it wasn't you then?"

"Because I was afraid they'd find out about Jewels, and think she was the one who did it."

"God love ya, you're a loyal mate. Is that the way people are in Newfoundland then?"

"Pretty much."

"Then I'll have to go there for sure."

We crested another hill, and Brian warned me to hold on tight because it might get rough on the way down. I didn't see how it could get any rougher than it already was, but it did. Every time we hit a bump or a rock, it was like getting kicked by a horse. We went downhill for what seemed like forever, faster and faster, sometimes sliding sideways, and I struggled not to think that we were going to crash. It would have helped if I had been able to see.

Finally, we reached the bottom, and Brian skidded to a stop. I could smell dust in the air, and the burning of the engine. It was working a lot harder than was good for it. Brian shut it off and suddenly there was silence. He told me I could sit up now. When I crawled out from under the seat, my head was spinning. We were hidden in a cloud of dust and dark shade. I had to wave the dust away from my face with my hat because there was no wind. "Where are we?"

"Beneath a bridge. On the river."

"Is there any water in the river?"

"No, none. Dry as a skeleton."

"Why are we stopping?"

"We'd be listening for that airplane. I want to make sure it doesn't see us drive up river. A few miles upstream from here and we're clear, mate. We'll just wait twenty minutes or so. That ought to do it."

So we sat, waited, and listened for the drone of an engine in the sky. But after a few minutes I just had to ask Brian something. I whispered. "Why did you come looking for me?"

"Aye. Well, Jewels told me about meeting you, before she flew back to Sydney. And then I saw on the news that they were looking for you, and I knew that you hadn't done it, so I just had to lend you a hand. I couldn't see a young fellah like yourself landing in prison for a crime you didn't commit. I'll be flying back to Sydney myself in a few days, just after I get a little fishin' in with some of my mates. This jeep belongs to one of them."

"I really appreciate that. But how did you know that it wasn't me who did it?"

"Well . . . let's just say I have an idea maybe I know who did. But the less we talk about that the better, don't you think? You can't be charged with conspiring to commit sabotage if you don't know who did it."

"Fair enough."

"All I knew for certain was that it wasn't you. And I couldn't sit around and watch you take the fall for it."

"Thank you for helping me out."

"Aye. I've got a feeling you'd do the same for me."

"I would."

"There you go. Have you got a plan then, Alfred?"

"I was going to wait a week or so, then sneak back to the pier, grab the sub, and disappear."

"Do you think maybe you're safer taking it now when they're thinking you're up here wanderin' around in the parks?"

"That's a good point."

"You're good at disappearing I take it."

"At sea I am."

"Where do you plan on going next?"

"Tasmania."

"Aye, that's a great place. I've got friends there you can stay with, if you'd like. But tell me, how do you plan on sneaking into the pier with the dog on your back?"

"I'll have to leave him on shore until I bring the sub up to the surface. Then I'll jump out and carry him in."

"But won't they see the sub when it's on the surface?"

"No. I'll bring the portal out of the water just a couple of inches. And I'll do it in the middle of the night. I'm not worried about being seen as much as being detected on radar."

"So, supposing you get your dog inside, and you're ready to go, how on earth do you sneak out of the harbour past the navy?"

"That's the tricky part. I have to wait for a boat or ship to pass close enough to the pier to pedal underneath it. I have a stationary bike hooked up to the driveshaft. It's slow, but undetectable by sonar. Once we're under a ship, I turn on the battery power and follow the ship out to sea. That's our best way to escape. We've done it before."

"I think maybe you should be working for the Special Forces, Alfred. Or maybe you *are* working for the Special Forces already, and you're not allowed to tell me. And that's a Special Forces dog you've got there in the bag. He sniffs out bombs and terrorists, does he?"

I laughed. "He probably could, but I wouldn't be willing to put his life at risk like that."

"Tell me, Alfred, does it have to be a big ship that you hide under, or will a motorboat do?"

"A motorboat would do, if it's big enough."

"Well, you're in luck then 'cause my mate's got one down at the marina, and I'll just have to ask him for the keys, and we're all set."

"Really? You wouldn't mind going to all that trouble?"

"Not at all, my son, not at all. I know you'd do the same for me if I were a Special Forces agent trying to escape the Australian navy."

"I would."

"But do you truly know what you're doing, attempting to escape right underneath their noses?"

"I have learned that sometimes the smartest thing to do is exactly what everyone assumes you'll never do, because people don't see what they're not expecting to see. Besides, I don't have a lot of choices."

"I suppose not. But how do you get into the submarine when it's sitting on the bottom? Have you got a special door underneath it then?"

"No. I go in through the hatch."

"On the top?"

"Yah."

"But doesn't the sea flood into it?"

"Yes, but I open and close it so quickly that only a couple of feet of water comes in, and the sump pumps take it out in ten minutes or so."

He turned and looked at me again. "You're serious?"

"Yes."

"But isn't it some bloody unnerving to open the hatch under water?"

"I'm getting used to it."

"You're not your average teenager, you must know that, do you, Alfred?"

"Yah, I guess so. But I don't know any other way to be."

"Aye. That'd be true for the lot of us."

Chapter Twelve

THE MOTORBOAT WAS A few feet shorter than the sub, but carried a tall cabin, and sat fat on the water, just fat enough to hide a small submarine from the air. If we could stay beneath her we could stay hidden. But it would take a lot of concentration to move at exactly the same speed. I would have to listen constantly for her motor. And though Brian would keep as steady a pace as possible, he'd have wind, waves and current to deal with. I would have just current.

We agreed to travel down the coast at eight knots. It would look less suspicious if Brian was not in a hurry. He would wear his fishing jacket and cap, and if we were discovered, would say he had no idea he was being followed by a submarine. I insisted upon that. It made no sense for both of us to get caught.

We parked the jeep by the marina after picking up the boat keys from Brian's friend. Brian didn't tell him anything, except that he was itching to fish for the day, which was true enough. He said that the less his friend knew the better, because he couldn't be accused of involvement in an action he truly knew nothing about. Brian sounded like a lawyer, too, but told me his job was constructing trains. He was the safety officer. Cool.

When we stepped from the jeep, I saw Seaweed on the pier, and felt tremendous relief. I wouldn't have known what to do if he hadn't shown up. I knew that birds had eyesight far superior to humans, but Seaweed's ability to track us from the air, even in a covered vehicle, boggled my mind.

It was the middle of the night when we climbed onto the boat, and dark still when we headed out of the marina and steered south, just like any other fisherman setting out early. Brian leaned his rods against the stern from where they could be seen. The plan was to stop very briefly by the breakwater, and make it look like he was checking something outside the cabin, just in case anyone was watching. I would slip over the side, swim down to the sub, open the hatch, and jump in. I'd pump air into the tanks and come up as quickly as possible, but I knew the sub would be sluggish because of the weight of the water. At exactly ten minutes Brian would rev the boat's engine and leave. I would have to be close enough beneath him to hear it and follow. If the sun were up he'd be able to see the sub beneath him, but it wouldn't be.

As we approached the breakwater, Brian signalled for me to get ready. Although I knew I had enough time, I was nervous. Opening the hatch under water was always nerve-wracking, but for some reason it was worse this time. I had told Seaweed to stay on the boat with Hollie, and I said it firmly three times, and hoped it would sink in. But he just looked at me and then turned his head. He would do what he wanted. If he flew back to the city, I didn't know how I'd ever get him back. Worrying about that was probably what was making me nervous.

On Brian's signal I took a few deep breaths, glanced at my watch, and went over the side. How I wished there was light, even a tiny bit, but it was pitch black. I might as well have had my eyes closed. It made it harder to find the sub, which wasn't exactly where I thought it was, but about fifteen feet away. It felt like forever until I found it. Eventually I struck the stern of the hull with my arm, then pulled myself along the side, up the portal, and spun open the wheel of the hatch. I was running out of air already, which was early, and was probably because I was more nervous than I should have been. As always, I had to fight down feelings of panic. It wasn't easy. Lifting the hatch felt harder, too. At the moment it was up, and I could feel the sea sucking downward from me, I had one of my worst panic feelings ever. My whole body resisted going inside the sub. It was rebelling against what felt like an act of suicide. I did manage to force myself down and inside, but lost probably two or three seconds hesitating, which meant a lot more water entered the sub before I pulled down the hatch and sealed it. I hung onto the ladder for a moment to collect my wits. My heart was pumping loudly in my head. There had to be an easier way to do this.

I jumped down the ladder into water up to my waist, waded over to the controls, and filled the tanks with air. The sub didn't move. I looked at my watch. Two minutes had passed. The sump pumps were going full blast. The emergency lights were on, and I could see. I stuck my hand against the wall at the water line and watched to see how quickly the water was dropping. It was too slow. Two minutes later I felt the sub lift very gently off the harbour floor. The water had fallen about eight inches below my hand. It was too slow! I had six minutes before Brian would leave, and there was nothing I could do but wait, stare at the depth gauge, and listen for the motor when Brian revved it. I couldn't turn on the sonar near the naval yard because they would hear it and know there was a submarine on the move.

Exactly six minutes later, I heard what sounded like a lawn mower above my head. It was distant through the steel hull, but was actually only ten feet away. I would have liked to have been closer, but time had run out. I engaged the batteries and followed the sound as well as I could.

It was hard at first, and I veered off-track a couple of times, but the further we went, the higher we rose, and the easier it became. At one point I felt the hatch very lightly bump the keel of the boat, and had to let a little water into the tanks. At least Brian knew we were beneath him. For the next five hours we would follow him like a giant remora underneath a small shark. The plan was to reach an area outside the three-mile zone, where Brian felt it was safe. Then he would rev the motor once again, and shut it off. I would surface awash, pick up Hollie and Seaweed, and continue on to Tasmania, another two thousand miles away.

It was a long and agonizing five hours. I had no way of knowing if Brian was being followed, either on the water, or in the air. He might not know, either. But five hours to the dot, he revved the engine once again, and shut it off. He was nothing if not precise. I shut the batteries, turned to portside, and pumped a little more air into the tanks. As we came up, I raised the periscope. It broke the surface into blazing sunlight. I saw the boat, Brian, Hollie, Seaweed, a distant freighter, and nothing else, so I surfaced awash beside them.

He was already handling his fishing rods when I opened the hatch, and even though he knew I was in a submarine, he looked shocked to see me.

"Bloody'ell! Have you ever been mistaken for a sea monster in that thing, Alfred?"

"Yah, once or twice."

"Well, I can understand that. But we got away, didn't we? The coast is clear."

I looked around. "I hope so. I don't know how many patrol

boats Australia keeps along the coast, or how closely they watch the water, so I'll have to be awfully careful."

"I think you'll do just fine, mate. I've never seen anybody with stealth like you. They'll be searching for you till the cows come home."

"I hope you're right."

"It's only a matter of time before they realize it wasn't you anyway."

"Do you think so?"

"Aye. They'll figure it out. In the meantime, you'll be long gone."

"We will."

Brian gave me the names and addresses of his friends in Tasmania, and said that he would give them a heads up that I might drop in, but wouldn't tell them exactly who I was, or how we were travelling. The less anyone knew the better. After I took Hollie and Seaweed on board, Brian and I shook hands, and I thanked him for his help.

"Not at all!" he said. "Jewels and I will be expecting you to visit us in Sydney, and we'll be deeply insulted if you don't show up."

"I'll do my best."

"Just park your sea monster down the coast a ways, give me a call, and I'll come and pick you up in my own jeep."

"Okay."

"Aye. Look after yourself now, my son, and have a fabulous sail to Tasmania."

"We will. Thank you again for all your help!" I climbed into the portal, waved one last time, closed the hatch, jumped down the ladder, and started up the engine. As we headed out past Australia's twelve-mile zone, I looked back through the periscope and saw Brian toss his fishing line into the sea. Thanks to him we were back on the water where we belonged. But once again I was an outlaw. I wondered who really had sabotaged the tanker, and how long I would be blamed for it. I had no idea but I sure was grateful to escape. I hoped the crew had enjoyed their shore leave, brief as it was; it would be another two weeks before we'd set eyes on land again.

Chapter Thirteen

FOR THE FIRST TIME at sea, we were hungry. I should have seen it coming, but didn't. It wasn't that we didn't have any food at all—we still had oats, potatoes, salt, sugar, spices, and tea—but we had run out of powdered milk, the potatoes had roots in them, and we had to eat porridge, without milk, three times a day. It was my own fault because I had never thought to stock up on fresh food before leaving Perth. We had left in too much of a hurry, and I didn't see how we could make land again until Tasmania; the risk of getting caught was too high. Once we rounded the southwest corner of Australia and entered the Great Australian Bight—an enormous bay half the size of the country—it was too far to return to shore anyway. If we followed the coast, which would be very foolish to do, our journey would take twice as long. So I set a course directly for Tasmania, and figured we'd just ration our food until we got there. With any luck, it would only take us a week.

But it took two. And our food was gone sooner than expected. Half of the potatoes weren't even eatable, the other half were tasteless, and Hollie's dog biscuits were finished. I fed the worst of the potatoes to Seaweed, who didn't care as much as we did, and shared the better ones, and my porridge, with Hollie. Still, after a few days, we were down to nothing but porridge.

I no longer felt much like riding the bike for exercise. Nor did Hollie care to run on his doggie treadmill. After a week, I stopped doing pull-ups on the bar in the portal. It quickly became obvious to me that when you didn't eat, you didn't have the energy to do anything. I spent a lot of time lying in bed, dreaming of food.

I was also a little concerned about our fuel. We should have had enough, except that with the current and wind against us we were burning more fuel than expected, and I had given all of our reserve fuel to Margaret. What made me nervous was that if we did run out of fuel, our only source of propulsion would be the stationary bike, which was terribly slow—about three or four knots—and wouldn't get us anywhere against a three-knot current. Without food I wouldn't have the energy to pedal anyway.

And so, at the end of two weeks, the sight of Tasmania was an emotional experience for me of a different sort. This time my tears were tears of relief, and I felt a strong urge to moor the sub somewhere secure, and spend at least a month on land, somewhere with nice trees, and nice people to talk to, and lots of shops with fresh food. Never again would I go to sea unprepared.

It would be hard to describe just how magical Tasmania seemed to me, though it sure wasn't easy to get ashore. Because I was exhausted, hungry, and feeling depressed—which is what happens when you are exhausted and hungry—it was surprisingly difficult to make smart decisions. I knew that I had to, and so I tried to force myself to act on the smartest thing to do, not on what I wanted to do. What I wanted to do was sail up the Derwent River into the city of Hobart, moor the sub, and find a restaurant. Instead, I spent a whole day and night searching for a place to hide the sub safely for at least a few days, so I wouldn't have to worry about it. I couldn't afford to be spotted. And I was in no condition to play a game of stealth with the coast guard or harbour police.

It was agonizing searching for the right spot, because the best ones were populated, and the unpopulated ones were too shallow or exposed, and at times I was so frustrated I just wanted to yell and scream. But that was my hunger talking. Hollie lay on his blanket with his head on his paws, watching me patiently. He had the patience of a saint. This was one time that I felt I had let him down, by running out of his

food and offering him nothing but oats, which he ate anyway, without enthusiasm. Seaweed left the sub at the first
sight of land, of course, and filled his belly with all the things
that seagulls liked to eat, which was everything. He would
return every few hours with a satisfied look on his face. But I
knew that whatever he was eating was not something we
would ever want to eat, no matter how hungry.

The spot I finally chose was in a tiny alcove on a peninsula
in the mouth of the Derwent River. As far as I could tell
through the periscope, half of the peninsula was covered
with houses, and the other half held trees and wild rocky
hills. The little alcove was below a steep cliff, above which
were a few small farms, nice homes, and an unmanned lighthouse called the Tinderbox.

The sea was rough against the cliff, and there was a strong
current and undertow, which made that part of the shore
completely unusable for pleasure craft and swimmers, and
therefore great for hiding a submarine. The rocky cliffs, tiny
coves, and gushing sea reminded me a lot of Newfoundland,
and made me feel homesick. But that was also my hunger
and exhaustion talking.

What was best about the spot I chose was that there were
tough, scraggly trees overhanging the water, which created a
perfect cover for the sub. Not only would they hide the portal
beneath their spidery branches, I could tie it securely to their
trunks, keeping it from scraping against the rocks, while
allowing for the rise and fall of the tide. The alcove wasn't a

whole lot bigger than the sub, but provided a great shelter from the waves. I didn't know what kind of trees they were but they had to be awfully tough to survive in the midst of crashing waves, wind, and salt.

It wasn't easy to climb out. The branches formed a thorny canopy that scraped my back as I lifted Hollie out in the tool bag, along with my tent, sleeping bag and knapsack. I also took a spare set of clothes. I didn't know how long we'd be gone, or if it would be cold at night, and I wanted to be prepared. Seaweed was gone when we hid the sub, and I doubted he'd be able to spot it beneath the trees. He'd find us along the road, though, or in the city, sooner or later. I felt confident about that.

Getting up the cliff was a lot harder than I had expected, too. I had the weight of the backpack, and Hollie in the tool bag as I gripped the rock with my hands and searched for safe crevices for my feet. It was so much harder because I had so little energy, and found it difficult to concentrate. I couldn't imagine how difficult life must be for people who are always hungry.

Slowly and carefully I made our way up the cliff in a diagonal direction, and entered a wooded area that could have been in Canada, if it weren't so dry. The more places around the world that I visited, the more I realized how wet Canada actually is, and especially Newfoundland.

Once we were in the trees, and turned to see the water, I felt another gush of emotion. But this time it was happiness and relief, and there were no tears. My belly was grumbling like a bear that had just come out of its cave in the spring. It knew that food was not far away. The centre of Hobart was ten miles, but we were only a mile or so from Blackman's Bay. I had seen it through the periscope, and knew that we would find food there. I bent down, let Hollie out of the tool bag, and we headed off through the woods like two escaped convicts.

Eventually we found a road, and followed it into the centre of Blackman's Bay. I knew it was possible that people might recognize us from the news back in Perth, but since that was over two weeks ago, I hoped that most people would have forgotten already. I wore my hat, and hadn't shaved since Perth, so I had a small stubbly beard that made me look a lot older, or so I thought, though it felt like I was wearing a wool sock on my face.

It was pleasant on the road. We started to see houses, and I thought they were incredibly beautiful, because I knew they had people and food in them. Then we started to see shops, and I saw a sign for a restaurant, just a small family restaurant, but I felt we had arrived in Heaven.

I carried Hollie in on my back, and left my knapsack outside behind a garbage can. A young woman met us inside the door, and showed us to a booth. I could smell food from the kitchen. I wanted to order everything they had on the menu. She asked me where I was from, and I said Sydney, and did my best to sound Australian. She asked me if I'd like to order something to drink before I looked over the menu, and I said I'd like two tall glasses of pop, a glass of milk, and a glass of water. She looked at me strangely. "You've been walking a while?"

"Aye."

Then I ordered a plate of spaghetti, a vegetable omelette, a spinach salad, apple pie and ice cream. The waitress grinned as she wrote it all down. "Do you want any potatoes on the side?" she said with a big smile.

"No, thank you." The one thing I had no appetite for was potatoes.

"You're going to stuff yourself, are you?"

"Aye."

"Are you going to share any of it with the little dog?"

I looked at Hollie staring up at us through the mesh, and I nodded.

"Okay then." And away she went. It felt like forever until she came back, and I had already started to nod off to sleep. The next thing I knew, she was standing beside the table, her arms loaded with plates. "Are you all right?" she said.

"Yes," I said, and forgot to use an Australian accent.

"You don't look so good. Were you lost in the woods or something?"

"No, we were just hiking a long way, and we're really hungry and tired. After this meal we'll be great."

She stood and stared as I opened the tool bag and let Hollie out. "Do I know you?" she said. "You look kind of familiar."

"I don't think so. We've never been here before."

"Why did you come?"

I picked up the knife and fork. I was hoping she would leave now so we could eat. I almost didn't care if she recognized us, and we had to run away, just as long as we could eat this meal first. "To become an environmentalist."

"Well, I'd say you've come to the right place for that. Enjoy your meal."

"Thank you, we will." I didn't think anybody ever enjoyed a meal more.

There was a TV hanging from the ceiling in one corner of the room, but I paid no notice to anything but our food for the first twenty minutes or so. Gradually, as my belly began to fill up, I started to glance at the TV more and more. Eventually I saw something on the screen that pulled me out of my seat. It was a harpoon shot from the bow of a ship, striking a whale. There was a lot of blood in the water. The screen showed dozens of whales bleeding on the deck of the ship, and blood pouring in steady streams into the sea. It was horrible. The screen shifted to a picture of a white bearded-man, with an angry scowl, standing in front of a ship. The ship was called the *Steve Irwin*. The words at the bottom of the screen read:

CAPTAIN PAUL WATSON OF THE SEA
SHEPHERD SOCIETY PREPARING TO LEAVE
HOBART HARBOUR FOR THE SOUTHERN OCEAN.

The photo had been taken just half a dozen miles away from where we were sitting. Boy, had we come to the right place.

Chapter Fourteen

AS SOON AS WE LEFT the restaurant, we headed towards the dockyard where the *Steve Irwin* was moored, where dozens of young men and women in black t-shirts were rolling barrels and carrying boxes and burlap sacks up a ramp. They were loading the ship by hand. They were clowning around a little, with a nervous energy, but looked dedicated. They were sailing to the Antarctic to risk their lives to save whales.

There were TV crews on the dock, and in one corner, by the bow of the ship, they were gathered around the captain. I recognized him from the photo. He was answering their questions but wasn't smiling. He was frowning, and looking impatient. He was older than everyone else there, but looked as though he had just stepped away from a fight to answer their questions.

Hollie and I walked as close to the ship as we dared. It fascinated me. It was painted with blue and grey camouflage, had scrapes and dents all over it, and looked as though it had been in a battle with a giant mechanical monster. But I knew, from what Jewels had told me, that it had been used to ram other ships. Jutting out of its sides were sharp iron blades, fitted to the hull specifically for ripping and tearing the hulls of whaling ships. This was no protest movement; this was a war.

I wasn't really worried that anyone would recognize us. Even if people remembered the incident in Perth, it was extremely unlikely they would remember what the suspects looked like from a single police sketch. So we walked around without fear. But we *were* recognized, I was sure of it, but by the person least likely to tell on us.

We had stopped just behind the camera crews, where the captain was being interviewed. I picked up Hollie because he was curious and wanted to see what was going on. The captain was wearing dark sunglasses, but at one point he took them off, stared hard in our direction, and his mouth curled into a smile. He stared right at us, and I knew that he knew. I raised my hand and waved. He raised his thumb and nodded ever so slightly. Suddenly, the cameras swung around, trying to see who he was smiling at. I bent down and let Hollie go, turned around, and walked away. It was pretty cool to see the captain. I had a feeling it wouldn't be the last time.

We went searching for the first person on Brian's list of friends—Merwin Hughes. Brian had said that Merwin was an inventor of sorts, and a dedicated environmentalist. He said he thought we would get along like two fish in a pond. I wasn't looking for a place to stay. I was just hoping that, if he were an inventor, he could help me convert the engine of the sub to burn vegetable fat instead of diesel fuel. It was something I had decided to do back in South Africa. I didn't know if he would be the right person to do it, but it was worth a try.

He lived in Claremont, about eight miles upriver from the centre of Hobart. I had to buy a map to find it. Hobart's harbour was fed by a river that quickly narrowed, as in Perth, but the city was much hillier, the roads were winding, and it was not as dry. It sat beneath Mount Wellington, a mountain with snow on its peak. It was the first time we had seen snow since sailing through the Arctic almost a year ago. The snow didn't make me feel homesick.

Now that our bellies were full, the walk felt miraculous, and I didn't mind if we didn't return to sea for a whole month. Hobart was friendly, welcoming, and beautiful, and there was a feeling of magic in the air, or maybe inside my head, I wasn't really sure, I was just so happy. I felt it strongest when we reached Merwin's house, and stood in front of the mailbox. It was fashioned in the shape of a man's head, cut and welded from rusty iron, with stars and crescent moons cut out of it, and a tall, bent, wizard's hat welded on top. It looked magical and ghastly at the same time. Rust has a way of doing that to metal.

The front of the house was low, and the back stretched down the hill, as if the whole thing were slipping slowly into the bay. There were trees on his property, and in between the trees were metal sculptures—finished ones, and partly finished ones. There were dinosaur-like creatures, animal-like creatures, lizards, and indescribable shapes that might have been just junk. It was hard for me to tell. On the side of the house, beneath a long tarp suspended between four trees, three old Volkswagen camper vans stood side by side like old friends from an earlier time—the "hippy" generation. With the sculpture, vans, odds and ends, Merwin's property stood out from all of his neighbours by a virtue I could relate to: it was really messy.

I went up to the door and knocked. Hollie was asleep in the tool bag but the knock woke him up. No one answered, so I knocked again. Still no one answered. I waited. Then, I figured there must be a workshop out back, and maybe he was in there. So, I went around the side, squeezed between the campers, stepped over a bit of junk, and found the back of the house. Sure enough, there was a large workshop tucked in behind the house, and there was a light on. It was part way down the hill towards the water. At the bottom was a boat-shed.

I could hear an electric tool running. It was the shrill

sound of metal cutting metal, a sound I knew well from the building of the sub. I went to the door, poked my head inside, and got a surprise. The shop was filled with strange creatures and machines, all cut and welded from metal. Some looked functional, and some looked scary, like monsters from a horror movie. At the very back, lying the length of the building, about twenty-five feet long, was a dragon. It had hinges and pulleys attached to its wings, and looked as though it was just sleeping, waiting for someone to walk in front of its mouth and wake it up. It looked so real I could imagine fire pouring from its nostrils. I was amazed.

I stood at the door, mesmerized by the dragon, until the cutter was shut off and the shop grew quiet. Then I heard a gentle but curious voice say "G'day? Can I help you?" I turned to see a short, middle-aged man standing in brown overalls and old-fashioned welder's goggles. He was almost bald, but the hair he had left was white and stiff with dust, and stuck out from his head like tinsel. He stood perfectly still, waiting for a response. At his feet, a large, bright orange cat suddenly appeared.

"Hi! My name is Alfred. Brian Bennett told me to look you up. He said he would call you about it."

He pulled off his goggles, lifted a pair of spectacles out of his pocket, and put them on. He frowned and shook his head. "No. . . . I don't think . . . wait now; he might have called. I haven't checked my messages for weeks. What did you say your name was?"

"Alfred."

"And why are you here?"

"I'm visiting Tasmania."

"From where?"

"Canada."

"That's a long way. And you're a friend of Brian's?"

"Sort of. We just met."

"Well, you must be friends if he told you to drop in on me. Come into the house and have some French toast. I was just about to make some. Do you like French toast?"

"Yes, but I don't want to impose."

"It's no imposition. We'll be glad to have company." He reached down and patted the cat. "This is Fritzi, the wonder cat."

I looked at the cat and wondered what made him a wonder cat. "Your dragon is very cool. It looks like it really flies."

Merwin turned around to look at the dragon, as if he didn't even remember it was there. "Nope. The motors flap the wings, throw the tail around, raise the head, open and shut the mouth, but that's it. It would take about a dozen rocket engines to get that thing into the air." He stared at the dragon as if he were considering the possibility.

"Do any of your sculptures actually work?"

He sighed. "A few of them do. I wish they all did. I started out making sculptures, and then was asked to design monsters for film, for special effects. I build them here, and ship them off to studios in Sydney. It's not a bad job, but I'm more interested in inventions that really work. My masterpiece is sitting down in the boathouse. Would you like to see it?"

"I would love to see it."

"Come on, I'll show you. Fritzi! My hat!"

Fritzi leapt onto a workbench, stretched up and grabbed Merwin's cap off a hook, and brought it back in his mouth. Merwin took it from him and put it on his head. It was a sandy-coloured hat with a faded golden dragon on the front. Now I knew why Fritzi was a wonder cat.

"He doesn't know he's a cat," said Merwin, patting Fritzi. "He thinks he's a dog."

"That's funny, I have a seagull who thinks he's an eagle," I said.

Merwin stared, bewildered, and I didn't think he believed me. He reached down and fed Fritzi a treat from his pocket, then patted him on the head again.

We followed him down to the boathouse. I kept Hollie in the tool bag the whole time because he was nervous around big cats. Merwin walked ahead, with Fritzi beside him. The boathouse was about the same size as the workshop, but sat on top of the water. We entered from one end, Merwin clicked on a light, and there, suspended in the air by cables, was an invention roughly the size of the dragon. At first glance I thought it *was* another dragon, except that it wasn't cut into moveable parts, it was just one piece. Yet it had what looked like wings, or fins. They were wide, webbed append-ages attached to bendable hydraulic arms. It had a tail made of discs, like a dinosaur spine, and one large moveable fin at the very back, as on a whale. There were several bubble windows, and it was hollow inside, with enough room for maybe two people. I would definitely want to see whatever film this creature was going to end up in. It was very, very cool.

"What is it?"

"What *is* it?" Merwin looked at me strangely, as if I should know what it was. "It's a submarine!"

Chapter Fifteen

IT WASN'T LIKE ANYTHING I had ever seen before. The fins resembled enormous duck feet on either side of a skinny whale. They looked funny, yet oddly seaworthy. I was dying to know if they really worked. "Do they work?"

"Of course. *Everything* works. That's the beauty of it. The fins are hydraulic, and they're made from titanium. They're hellishly strong, but lightweight. Come inside and I'll show you."

I followed Merwin up a stepladder and squeezed through a narrow portal hidden inside a dorsal fin. That was cool. I had to pull Hollie off my back to get inside. The sub swung side to side as we climbed in. Then we had to crouch down because there wasn't enough room to stand. The hull was made of steel, which Merwin had cut and welded expertly, but hadn't painted, insulated, or lined with wood, so it was pretty rough. It really felt like we were inside the stomach of a sea monster.

"You sit here, put your feet there, and pull back on the levers the way you'd row a boat. The webbed paddles open up against the water on the backstroke, then fold together like bat wings and rush to the front on the forward stroke, then open again on the backstroke. The hydraulic arms give you a powerful stroke."

"It looks awesome. Have you tested it in the water yet?"

"No."

"I see you have an engine, too."

"Yeah."

"Does it burn vegetable fat?"

"It does."

"Is there a propeller?" I didn't see one.

"It's underneath the tail. It's just a small one."

I stared all around. There was nothing as fascinating to me as a submarine, especially one with mechanical invention. I couldn't help wondering what this thing would look like cutting through the water. What would whales and dolphins think? What would the coast guard think? "What will you use it for?"

Merwin rubbed his hands together anxiously. "My dream

is to join the Sea Shepherd Society, and help save whales, but I know that's probably unrealistic in a vessel this size. If this proves seaworthy, I'll make a bigger one."

"Cool. Where are your air compressors?"

Merwin looked surprised that I asked that. "It's here." He pointed to a blue tank. It was pretty small.

"Is there only one?"

"Yeah. Why would you need more than one?" He looked a little confused.

"For safety. Do you have a heating system?"

"A heater? No, I didn't think to put in a heater. I figured I'd just dress warmly. I suppose a heater's not a bad idea." He took a notepad out of his pocket and scribbled it down.

"The ocean gets really cold. What about an air-conditioner?"

"An *air-conditioner*? Why on earth would you need an air-conditioner inside a submarine?"

"Because of the sun, and the heat of the engine, and to circulate the air."

Merwin looked at me strangely, then wrote it down in his notepad. I looked around some more. "Where are your batteries?"

"There aren't any. That's why I have the hydraulic paddles. I'll use the engine on the surface, and the paddles when I submerge. I don't see the need to complicate things with batteries. I don't like the idea of running electricity inside a submarine."

That meant that the sub could only move under water

when he rowed. But what if he broke his arm when he was at sea? Or what if he got sick, or ran out of food, like we had, and had no energy? And I guess he wasn't concerned about speed. The duck fins looked pretty cool, but they'd be awfully slow. He hadn't tested them in the water yet anyway, so he didn't even know if they worked.

"What about your casings? These ones are just temporary, are they?" Everywhere that he had cut holes in the hull—for windows, paddle arms, and valves—were casings that might have been suitable for a machine on land, to keep the dust and rain out, but none of them would hold up against water pressure for more than a few seconds. They looked really neat, like out of a spaceship movie, but if he ever went to sea in this submarine, he would drown before he got out of sight of his boathouse.

"What's wrong with my casings?" He looked a little wounded.

"They won't keep the sea out. You'll drown." I hated to be so critical, but he didn't appear to realize how dangerous it actually was to go under the water in a machine. The sea doesn't care if you are sincere, and it doesn't care what your submarine looks like. It only cares if it's watertight.

Merwin stared at me intensely: partly curious, partly defensive. "How come you know so much about submarines, Alfred?"

I hesitated. "Because I live in one."

"You're kidding."

I shook my head. "Did you hear about an incident in Perth a couple of weeks ago, where a tanker was sabotaged, and everyone thought it was someone in a submarine?"

"Yeah, of course. Everybody has seen that. It was big news."

"Well, the guy they're looking for is me."

His mouth dropped. "No."

"Yes, but I didn't do it. Honestly. Somebody else did; but I don't know who."

"But . . . you travel in a submarine?"

"Yes. I've been living in one for a couple of years now. It's my home."

Merwin looked stunned. Then he drifted off in a trance, probably lost in his imagination, and it took him quite a while to come back. I leaned against the inside of the hull with one arm, and held Hollie in the tool bag with the other. The sharp, biting odour of metal reminded me of Ziegfried's workshop back in Newfoundland, where we had built the sub. Then Hollie sneezed, and Merwin snapped out of his trance. "Boy, have we got things to talk about, Alfred. Please come in and have French toast with me."

"Okay." That sounded pretty good to me.

So we climbed out and followed him back up the hill to his house, which was even messier inside than out. But it was cosy. And Merwin made probably the best French toast in the world. He bought the bread from an organic bakery, the eggs from an organic farm where the hens had the run of the place; the milk from cows that were grass fed; the salt, cinnamon, butter, and yogurt from a local organic store. Everything was organic, and grown or made in Tasmania, except the brown sugar, which was imported, but was organic, too. I had never had yogurt on French toast before, and was kind of doubtful, until I tried it. Then, I couldn't stop eating it. While we ate, Merwin asked me a lot of questions about my experiences in the sub, and I answered them, including telling him how I was hoping he might be able to convert the engine to burn vegetable fat.

After a while, Hollie had to go outside. "I have to let my dog out to use the bathroom," I said. "I'll be right back."

"Okay."

I opened the back door and let Hollie out. "Don't go far, Hollie. Just scratch on the door when you want in, okay?" Hollie looked up at me as if to say, "When are we leaving this place?"

"Soon," I said, and went back inside.

When I sat down, Merwin looked alarmed. "Did you let that little dog outside by himself?"

"Yes. Why?"

"Fritzi's out there. He hates dogs. He gets very aggressive around them. He'll hurt a little dog like that. You'd better hurry."

I jumped up. The next thing we heard was a cat hissing loudly, Hollie barking, and a terrible sound of animals fighting in the yard. We rushed out. "I'm sorry," Merwin said. "I should have warned you about Fritzi."

I searched for Hollie in the dark, and saw him running over from a tree. He looked okay to me. But Fritzi was up in the tree. At the trunk of the tree was Seaweed, his wings spread almost five feet across, his beak wide open, like a giant lobster claw. Fritzi was clinging to the branch, hissing in fright. Merwin was frightened, too. "What the heck is that?"

"I'm sorry," I said. "That's Seaweed. He's my first mate. I should have warned you about him. He hates cats."

"What kind of bird is *that*?"

"A seagull."

"He doesn't look like any seagull I've ever seen, he looks like a monster!"

"Sorry about that. Seagulls from Newfoundland are bigger than the ones around here. And Seaweed has always been really aggressive. I don't know why. He's very protective of Hollie. They've been through a lot together." I went over and tossed Seaweed a dog biscuit I had in my pocket. He gobbled it up, folded his wings, and twisted his head at me, looking for more.

"That's your crew?"

"Yes."

"Wow."

Merwin helped Fritzi down from the tree and put him in the shop. I brought Hollie back into the house. Seaweed went up on the roof. We came back to the table, sat down, and continued eating. Merwin was quiet for a while. I could tell he was thinking about something. I shared my French toast with Hollie. By the time we had finished eating, Merwin said he had an offer to make me. He sounded serious.

"Okay?"

"Here's my offer, Alfred. You take me out on your submarine, and teach me everything you know about submarines, and I'll convert your engine to burn vegetable fat, and teach you everything I know about environmentalism. What do you think?"

I sat back in my seat. It was an interesting offer, but I had to think about it. I had a rule about not taking passengers on my sub, except for emergencies, because I didn't feel I could truly protect them. The sea was too dangerous. On the other hand, it *would* be very helpful if Merwin taught me everything he knew about environmentalism. And I did want to convert the engine to burn vegetable fat.

I'd have to think about it. As captain, I was responsible for all passengers and crew on my sub. That was the law of the sea, and I explained it to Merwin. He listened carefully, but had a quick answer. "Okay, but look at it this way: I am the captain of another submarine, in training, and I am requesting your help in order to be safer at sea. Doesn't that put me in a special category?"

It was a good point. But there was something else: Merwin was probably sixty years old. I was just turning seventeen. If he came on my submarine, he would have to obey my orders. Could he do that? He nodded his head and said no problem.

I still didn't know. I told him I'd have to think about it.

"Fair enough. Where's your submarine anyway, Alfred?"

"In a tiny cove, in the mouth of the harbour. It's hidden."

"Why don't you bring it up here? Would it fit in the boat-house?"

"It might."

"What do you think?"

"I don't know. Can I sleep on it?"

"Of course. Would you like the couch?"

"No, thank you. We'll be more comfortable outside. We've spent so much time at sea lately; anywhere on land is nice."

"I envy you. It must be nice to spend so much time at sea. Pick any spot you like, but watch out for sharp edges of the sculptures in the dark. I can tell that you're a cautious fellow, Alfred. Were you always like that, or did you learn that at sea?"

"I learned it at sea."

"I suppose I'd have to learn it, too."

I nodded. He sure would.

Hollie and I slept under the stars. My belly was so full I couldn't even remember the hungry feeling I had had for the past week. Hollie climbed onto the bottom of the sleeping bag, lay flat the way he sometimes lay in the sun, and went into a deep sleep. Seaweed appeared a little while later. I heard the rush of his feathers just before I drifted off.

I slept well, except for a couple of times when I woke to see the stars shining between the pointy treetops, and fell back to sleep with a pleasant feeling. But then, I had a bad dream. It was probably because I had eaten too much. I dreamt that

Merwin was in the sub in the middle of a storm. He was panicking in the small space, trying to escape. He climbed up the ladder and opened the hatch. I yelled at him to come back down, but he wouldn't listen. Then he climbed out, fell overboard, and drowned. I woke with the image of his body drifting away, and a strong feeling that it would not be a good idea to agree to his plan. I'd be happy to share whatever I could about submarines, and grateful for whatever he could teach me about the environment, but we'd have to do it on land. Besides, Hollie and I really needed a break from being at sea.

But when I told Merwin my decision, he was ready for me again. He didn't take no for an answer.

"Alfred?"

"Yes?"

"You've come here to become an environmentalist, right?"

"Right."

"And that's because the oceans are in trouble and need our help, right?"

"Right."

"Because we're destroying them, aren't we?"

"Yes, I guess so." Where was he going with this?

"Okay then, how can it make sense for you to worry about my safety when the oceans and the whole world is being destroyed? What's the point of trying to save my life if we're going to lose everything anyway? Wouldn't it make more sense to help me become a more effective environmentalist, too, danger and all?"

How could I argue with that? He was right. Why did I feel so responsible for his safety anyway? He was a grown man; he ought to be able to look after himself.

"Okay. You're right. I will agree to your plan."

"You *will*? Great!"

"I just need to know a couple of things first."

"Okay. Shoot."

"Do you have claustrophobia?"

"No."

"Can you swim?"

"Yes."

"Very well, or just a little?"

"I'm a strong swimmer."

"When was the last time you went swimming?"

"I don't know, maybe ten years ago. What's that got to do with sailing a submarine?"

"Everything." He was not a strong swimmer; he was out of shape. "If you come to sea with us, you'll have to swim. Your life will depend on it. If you're not in good shape, you might drown."

"That may be so, but that's a risk I am willing to take."

Yah, I thought to myself, but I'm the one who will have to deal with your dead body.

"You're thinking it will be harder than it will be, Alfred."

I shook my head. "You're thinking it will be easier than it will be."

Chapter Sixteen

BEFORE WE COULD GO anywhere, we had to pick up the sub, stock it with food, and fill it with fuel, which I was hoping would be vegetable fat once Merwin had modified the engine to burn it. I hoped that wouldn't be too difficult to do. Though he was highly skilled at making machinery look amazing, I didn't know if he was any good at making it work. If his choice of casings were any example, then I'd say we were in trouble. But perhaps he just had no experience with water pressure. In the back of my mind, I knew that Ziegfried wouldn't be pleased to know that anyone was fiddling around with the engine of the sub that he had built, and I knew that

I had to tell him before we did anything, which I planned to do from a phone booth on my way back to the sub. But first, we would go for a ride in one of the vans, and I would have a chance to see a vegetable-fat engine in action, which I was really keen to do.

So we climbed into one of the old campers, and Merwin turned the key. But nothing happened except a sound like a marble dropping and rolling through a gumball machine. Merwin didn't seem concerned. Suddenly the engine shook, banged, and rattled like an old cow with a cold. It coughed and wheezed, and then belched out a cloud of blue smoke that completely hid the trees behind us.

"She's a little shaky to start," said Merwin. He was shouting over the noise. "Once she warms up, we can switch from diesel to fat."

"You mean, you're burning diesel now?"

"Yeah, you have to start with diesel, otherwise you'll clog up the motor. Vegetable fat has a thick viscosity; it has to run hot. You have to run diesel before you shut it off, too"

"But . . . doesn't the engine burn only vegetable fat once you convert it?"

"No, you have to burn both. You have two tanks: one for fat; one for diesel."

I didn't like the sound of that. I didn't like the cloud of blue smoke either. "Your engine sounds clogged *now*. When was the last time you cleaned it?"

"Cleaned it? Never. Don't worry; the blue smoke will burn

off after a bit. She'll run well enough once she's out on the road."

But she didn't. She stalled four times in the yard. So we pushed her out to the road, jumped in, and coasted downhill while Merwin popped the clutch to start her.

"She's been sitting awhile," said Merwin as we went noisily down the road.

We hadn't gone far when he suddenly swerved to the side of the road, hit the brake, and skidded to a stop. The engine promptly stalled.

"Why did you stop?"

"Snails."

"What?"

"On the road. Do you see all those little rocks on the road?"

"Yes?"

"Those are snails. Come on, let's lift them off the road."

"Are you serious?"

"Of course." Merwin flicked his emergency blinkers on, jumped out of the camper, and started picking up snails. I joined him.

"They come out after a rain. Why they want to cross the road, I don't know. But if we don't pick them up, they'll get run over."

I looked down the road and saw what looked like bits of gravel that had fallen off the back of a truck. They stretched for as far as I could see. "But we can't pick up snails all day?"

"No, but we can save a lot of them. Some of the snails of

Tasmania are endangered."

"Are these ones?"

"No, I don't think so. Not yet anyway. But a little preven-
tion goes a long way."

And so, for a little over two hours, Merwin and I walked
along the road picking up snails. Often a car would come by
and run over them, crushing their shells. But we saved hundreds, that is, unless they crawled back up the bank and onto
the road. We had to push the camper to get her going again,
and left a fat cloud of blue smoke in our wake. At least the
engine was burning vegetable fat, not diesel, once it was
warmed up; and that was supposed to be better for the environment.

In Hobart, we picked up five heavy pails of smelly, deep-
fried fat from a restaurant. The cooks at the restaurant gave
Merwin the fat for free. We loaded the pails into the camper
and headed back. Merwin never turned the motor off, for
fear it would stall. He drove the van like a bus driver, swinging his arms in wide circles.

"We'll heat the fat in the shop and strain it. Then it'll be
good to burn."

"Can you tell me again why it is better to burn vegetable
fat?" I needed to hear it again because the clouds of smoke we
were leaving everywhere were bothering me. How could this
be better for the environment?

"Because we don't have to drill it out of the ground. We
don't have to cause environmental damage and oil spills, and

we don't have to kill animals, birds, and fish in our hunger to get it. Vegetable fat is even better than biodiesel because it has already been used once to feed us, and a second time to give us energy."

"Oh. I just wish we weren't leaving a trail of blue smoke everywhere we go."

"Yeah, an electric motor would be great, but the power has got to come from somewhere. And most of the electricity in the world is generated from burning coal, which is the dirtiest of all fuels."

"I know. I saw a protest about it in Perth."

"We're lucky in Tasmania because we get most of our power from hydroelectric dams on our rivers, and wind turbines, although those technologies have their problems, too. They wanted to build the Franklin Dam back in the seventies, but it would have created a lake and flooded forests, animal habitat, and ancient aboriginal art. So a bunch of us protested hard against it, and they threw us in jail. But in the end, we won." Merwin smiled. "That was the start of the environmental movement here."

He pointed to a faded photograph on the dash that showed a young man with a beard, long black hair and a headband, being handcuffed by police. "That's me. I was a hippy then."

"Cool." I wondered if he realized he still looked like a hippy.

We came around a sharp turn, and started down a long hill. On the right was a clearing between trees. Merwin got excited when he saw it. "I want to show you something."

"Okay."

We turned off the road onto a dirt lane, drove about half a mile into the foothills of Wellington Mountain, into a dry clearing that looked out of place with the lush mountain above it. It reminded me of Africa. Without shutting off the motor, Merwin got out and walked over to a mound of dirt about three feet off the ground. I followed him. "There," he said.

"What is it?" It just looked like a pile of dirt to me.

"Look."

I took a few steps closer. "Oh! It's an ant hill."

"Yeah."

"The whole thing?"

"Yeah."

"Wow. That's amazing."

"Sometimes, when I'm frustrated, I come here and just watch the ants work."

"Really?"

"Yeah. It relaxes me. Each ant carries a tiny piece of earth on its back. You can watch them for hours and you won't see any change in the size of their hill. But if you come back two weeks later, you will."

"Cool."

We stood and watched the ants crawl in and out of the top of the mound. They were so tiny it was hard to believe they had really built it. Merwin turned and started back towards the van. "And that pretty much sums up my philosophy of environmentalism."

I nodded, but didn't really know what he was talking about. I'd have to think about it.

Chapter Seventeen

EARLY THE NEXT MORNING, Hollie and I hiked back to the sub. Merwin offered to drive us, but I said we'd rather walk. I couldn't bear the thought of blowing dirty engine smoke all the way down to the Tinderbox lighthouse. I'd rather walk for ten hours than pollute the air for one.

It was a great walk. The air was fresh and cool, and reminded me a little of Newfoundland, without the fog. Seaweed joined us at the start, but disappeared as soon as the leftover French toast was gone. Hollie and I settled into our long distance pace. The more we walked, the happier we were. Sometimes, lying on my bed in the sub, I'd dream of walking across deserts, jungles, and mountain ranges, and I'd fantasize that if we weren't sailing around the world in a submarine, we'd be walking around it. Probably after a couple of weeks, though, we'd be dreaming of going to sea.

On the way, I thought over the deal we had made. I had agreed to take Merwin on the sub only because of what I was trying to learn, but, in truth, I wasn't really happy about it. The sub would get crowded fast with somebody else on board. And what if he snored, or talked too much, or got seasick? And what if he wouldn't obey my orders, or went crazy and tried to take control of the sub? I knew that captains of military airplanes and subs used to carry pistols, and had the authority to shoot anyone who disobeyed a direct order or threatened the ship. That was pretty severe, but there was a reason for it. What if a person went berserk, sank a sub, or crashed a plane, and killed everyone? I knew I was worrying too much, but couldn't stop my imagination from running away with it. The sub was a small, confined space, and a dangerous place to be if anything went wrong. And something always went wrong at sea, sooner or later. That was one of the unwritten rules.

But I had agreed because I believed what Merwin had said was true—it was more important to save the environment than it was to worry about protecting someone who didn't even want protecting. And it wasn't as if he would sail with us forever. We'd just travel along the coast for a couple of weeks, and I'd make a point of stopping and sleeping on land as much as possible. That wouldn't be so bad.

We followed the winding roads downtown, and passed the

dockyard where the *Steve Irwin* had been moored, but she was gone. She'd be on her way to the Antarctic now. Tasmania was only two thousand miles away from Antarctica, due south, and many research and expedition vessels were stationed here, including the *Aurora Australis*, a huge icebreaker painted as red as a raspberry. We walked right past it. Having come through the Arctic, and run into polar bears, snowy owls, and treacherous ice chunks; having fallen into icy water, and been trapped in the ice for three unbearably long days, I had no desire to visit Antarctica on this trip. I knew well enough what ice and icebergs looked like.

But the Sea Shepherd Society was on its way to save whales, and that was more than worth the trouble. I didn't know why Merwin didn't just join their crew if he wanted to help save whales, unless . . . he was too old. I remembered how young the crew on the dock had been. Yah, that was probably it. It was a very physically demanding job, and it was dangerous. I sure hoped he didn't think we were sailing the sub into Antarctic waters, because we weren't.

On the far side of the dockyard, I found a phone booth, squeezed inside with Hollie, and dialled the operator. She helped me make the long-distance call to Ziegfried. It was the evening of the day before in Newfoundland. When I heard Ziegfried's voice in the receiver, my heart rushed into my throat. I never knew why my emotions always snuck up on me.

Ziegfried was my best friend and mentor. He had designed and built the sub, with me helping as his lackey—sanding, filing, and searching for materials in the junkyard. Ziegfried was a giant of a man, but had the most generous heart, and it was only because of his generosity, and inventive genius, that I had been able to go to sea in a submarine. Over the two and a half years it had taken us to build and test the sub, he had become like a father to me.

We had an agreement that I would be the captain of the sub whenever she was in the water, but he had the right to dry-dock her whenever he felt she wasn't safe anymore, for whatever reason. Once she was out of the water, he was the boss. And he was obsessed with safety. I mean, I knew he had to be, and that was why I was still alive, but it could be painful waiting until he felt the sub was ready to go back in the water. She was due for a servicing, too, which meant that I should have been sailing back to Newfoundland now, where we would haul her out of the water, scrape the barnacles off, sand her down, and give her several new coats of paint. Then, we would start on the engine and other systems inside. I was nervous even calling him, because I was afraid he'd say it was time to turn around and come home, where I didn't yet want to go. But I had to tell him about converting the engine to burn vegetable fat. I'd be breaking our agreement if I didn't.

"Al! It's so great to hear from you, buddy! We were worried. We heard about the incident with the tanker in Perth."

"You did?"

"Yes. It was on the national news. Tell me you weren't involved."

"I wasn't."

"I knew it!"

"I mean, I was there, but I didn't do it."

"Of course you didn't. And now you're in Tasmania?"

"Yah. How is Sheba and everybody else?"

"Sheba's great. Everybody's great. It's so good to hear from you, Al. Your grandfather asks if you are coming home. What can I tell him?"

"Uhh . . ."

"I didn't think so. You know, we're going to have to raise the sub into the boathouse sometime soon, and give her a good overhaul."

"I know."

"We don't want to wait too long."

"I know. Actually, I met an inventor here who says he can convert the engine to burn vegetable fat. What do you think? Wouldn't that be a good thing?"

There was a long pause. I held my breath.

"Interesting, Al. Who is he? Is he an engine specialist?"

"Not exactly. He's . . . an inventor and a sculptor."

"A sculptor?"

"Yah. But he converted the engines of his VW campers to burn vegetable fat. I had a ride in one yesterday."

There was another pause. "How did it run, Al? Did it burn cleanly?"

"Not exactly."

"Al . . ."

"But it's great for the environment."

"Al . . ."

"And he gets the fat for free from the restaurants here."

"That's great, Al, but vegetable fat will ruin a good engine. Did it burn clean, or did you leave a trail of smoke?"

This wasn't going as well as I had hoped. "It was pretty smoky."

"Did he have special fuel injectors for the fat, or did he use a two-tank system?"

"He uses two tanks."

"And he has to heat up the fat?"

"Yah."

"You don't want to go that way, Al. You'll clog up the engine in no time. And you don't want anybody touching the engine who doesn't have a lot of experience. You can't afford to have an engine breakdown at sea, you know that."

"I know."

We were both silent.

"Tell you what, Al: wait till you come back, and we'll do it here. And we'll do it properly. Then you can burn all the vegetable fat you like. Okay?"

I was disappointed, but knew that Ziegfried was right. "Yah, okay."

"Does he have any experience with submarines, Al?"

"He's building one right now."

"Is he? Would you go to sea in it?"

"No."

"There's your answer right there, Al."

"Yah, I know."

"Just so we're clear on this: nobody's going to touch the engine but you, correct?"

"Yah. Correct."

"Good then. Al, Sheba wants to talk. I'll put her on. I miss you, buddy."

"I miss you, too."

Sheba was married to Ziegfried, but I had met her first when she lived alone on her own little island in Bonavista Bay, with a house full of living creatures. To the dozens of rescued animals, birds, reptiles, bugs, and plants of all sorts that she had been taking in for years, she was Mother Nature. She was the most loving person you could ever possibly meet. In all of my travels I have never met anyone as wonderful as her. Her home has become my home when I'm not at sea.

I last saw Sheba and Ziegfried in India, where they came for their honeymoon, just a few months earlier.

"Alfred, my precious boy . . . my heart is heavy . . . I am missing you."

"I miss you, too."

"You sailed to Australia instead of coming home."

"I know, I'm sorry."

"It must be the right thing because you are following your heart."

"I'm learning about environmentalism here."

"Yes, I know. You are a warrior for peace. I have been reading your cards, and have had dreams about you."

Yikes! Whenever Sheba had dreams about me, dangerous things happened, and I had to watch my step. She was an oracle. If she told you something was going to happen, it would.

"What did you dream?"

I heard her sigh on the other end of the phone. That wasn't a good sign, either. I could see her standing by the bookcase in her cottage home, surrounded by ocean and fog, but basking in the generated light that helped her hydroponic garden grow. There were probably a couple of cockatiels on her shoulder, a goat nibbling at the hem of her skirt, and a butterfly or two in her hair—her long, red hair, shaped with a thousand seashell curls, like waves on the sea. Sheba was the queen of the sea, too.

"You will be hurt where you have been hurt before, Alfred, but you will come out of it. That is the important thing, and that is all I know. I am not worried for you, my dear heart, because I know you are dedicated to coming home, and my dreams tell me you will indeed come home."

"That's good. What kind of injury do you think it will be?" I had been shot in the arm a year ago; I sure hoped it didn't mean I'd get shot again.

"I don't know. It might not be of the body; it might be of the heart."

"Oh. That's strange. But I will be okay?"

"Yes, my precious one. I would protect you so that you would not bruise your toe against a stone, but you are a man, and you must follow your heart. And how are our furry and feathered children?" She meant Hollie and Seaweed.

"They're great. Lots of long walks here. Everybody's doing great."

"My heart is lifting. I love you with all my heart, Alfred."

"I love you, too."

"That is all I needed to hear. I am happy now."

Sheba did not shy away from expressing what was in her heart. But now I had to wonder what was coming my way. Whatever it was, I sure hoped it wasn't because I had agreed to take Merwin on the sub.

Chapter Eighteen

IT WAS TWILIGHT BY the time we reached the Tinderbox lighthouse. We had stopped for pizza and snacks along the way. Getting down the cliff was easier than getting up, but it was still difficult, especially with Hollie on my back, and the pack, which threw off my balance. I wouldn't have been so afraid of falling if I knew we would land in the water, but we wouldn't have. And I couldn't help wondering about each danger now, if it was what Sheba had predicted. It was a relief to get down to the water, where the trees were still covering the sub, and the sub was waiting faithfully, like an old friend. I hadn't planned on coming back so soon, but was glad for the opportunity to hide the sub inside a boathouse. It would be much safer there if the coast guard and navy were still watching for us, which they probably were.

I untied the ropes from the tree trunks, raised the branches above the hatch, and squeezed inside. Even though we had only been away for a couple of days, and I wasn't anxious to return to sea, it was nice to be back inside our own space. Hollie trotted happily over to his blanket, circled a few times, and plopped down. I lifted the pizza and bottle of milk out of my bag, and put the milk into our little fridge. Then I put on a pot of tea. It would be nice to have fresh milk in my tea, and Hollie and I could snack on the pizza on the way up the river.

But after crossing an ocean, sailing up a river was kind of unnerving, and took a lot of concentration. After sailing in water with nothing to run into in any direction—where I could set our course and lie down and sleep—sailing in water where I had to pay close attention every single second, or risk hitting something, or running aground, felt like crawling through a drainpipe without being allowed to touch the sides.

We didn't sail up by ourselves though. I waited a few hours until a larger vessel turned into the mouth of the river and headed upstream. Then I steered out from the bank, tucked in close behind, and followed her like a shadow, invisible to radar and sonar because of her size and the noise of her engines. I took a good look at her first though. I wouldn't make the mistake I made in India—sailing behind a naval frigate and getting depth-charged.

She was a freighter called the *Zinc Fairy*, and she ushered us right past the centre of Hobart, and underneath the first of two bridges that we had to pass before reaching Merwin's boathouse. This was the famous Tasman Bridge that had been hit by a freighter back in 1975, knocking a big chunk out of the bridge, which fell onto the ship and sank her, killing twelve people. The river was well over a hundred feet deep here, and that freighter still lay where she settled.

We followed the *Zinc Fairy* below the surface, until she docked at a refinery just north of the bridge. I watched through the periscope the whole time, keeping tightly in her wake. Any waterway with room enough for her had room enough for us so long as we stayed in her wake. It took only about an hour altogether, but the vibrations of her engines rattled our teeth and shook our bones. It wasn't fun playing shadow with a freighter.

The trickiest moment came when she was approached by two tug boats that helped her turn and moor. Even in a slow and easy current—just four knots—it must have been a challenge to turn a freighter right around, and line her up neatly against a dock. I waited until their lines were attached and they were busy tugging her before I flicked on the sonar, sank twenty feet, and headed upriver. By the time anyone could guess there was a small submarine in the river (if anyone was even listening), and came looking for us, we'd be safely hidden in Merwin's boathouse.

It was after midnight when I spotted the boathouse through the periscope. It was the only one in the bay. Few people had need of a boathouse in this climate, I supposed. And the houses along the river, although nice enough, were not the luxurious mansions you'd see in some places. Merwin's boat-house was plain, unlike his sculpture, and blended in with the background so that you wouldn't even notice it unless you were looking for it. You certainly wouldn't think that it was hiding a submarine, and was about to hide another one.

Merwin was sitting on the deck, staring at the water. Fritzi was curled up beside him. Merwin knew that we'd be coming sometime in the night, but not exactly when. I wondered how long he had been waiting there. Would he have sat and waited all night? I bet he would have.

Though he was staring at the water, there was no way he could spot the periscope in the dark. There was light from the moon and stars, but the periscope was hard to spot even in the day, even when you were looking for it. I came to about fifty feet in front of him, stopped, and very slowly rose until the hatch was jutting above the surface about a foot. Still, he didn't see us. I climbed the portal and opened the hatch as quietly as I could. He never moved. He was staring in our direction but didn't see us. Maybe he was in a trance, dream-ing of inventions. I didn't want to alert any of his neighbours so I quietly called out to him. "Merwin."

He lifted his head a bit, saw me, and jumped to his feet. "Alfred! There you are!"

"Shhhhh!" He was practically yelling.

He lowered his voice. "Sorry. This is so exciting! I'm so

glad you made it. Was it difficult coming up the river?"

I shook my head. "It was okay. But the sooner we hide the sub, the better. It's pretty shallow here. How much clearance is there under your sub exactly?"

"Five feet, I think, allowing for the tide, which rises about four feet. I could probably raise my submarine another foot or two."

"No, that should be good enough. If you open the doors, I'll bring her in. Better keep the lights off though."

"Right-o!" Merwin swung open the boathouse doors. I pumped a little air into the tanks, rose a few more feet, and motored very gently inside. It was a tight squeeze. The hull squealed along the wooden deck as we went in. Fortunately the tide was out, so the sub above us did not bang my head. But what a weird feeling: like squeezing into a wooden body suit. Once we were inside, Merwin shut the doors, flicked the switch, and flooded the boathouse with light.

"Well done, Alfred. Well done!"

"Thank you. I don't know if we were detected. I don't think so. We weren't followed anyway."

Merwin stared at the sub like a kid seeing a Christmas tree for the first time. I could relate.

"Can I have a look inside?"

"Sure."

He reached over, grabbed a handle, and pulled himself onto the hull. He didn't jump like a younger person would have. I went down the ladder to make room for him. He came down the ladder slowly, staring in wonder. "Wow . . . there's so much equipment."

I looked around. I was so used to it I hardly noticed. "Yah, I guess so."

"It's a lot more complicated than I expected."

I nodded.

"You've got a bicycle rigged up to the driveshaft!"

"Yah. It's pretty slow, but it works great in emergencies. Gives me a lot of exercise, too."

"Amazing." His eyes pored over the pipes, valves, gauges and casings that ran along the walls, the ceiling, and under the floor. He saw the control panel, radar and sonar screens, the periscope, and observation window. He turned and saw my hanging cot, and the doors to the engine and storage compartments. The engine door was open. "Do you really need all of this to go to sea?"

I nodded again. "Yup."

"And yet it's lined with wood. It's beautiful."

"Thank you."

"It looks comfortable."

"She is."

"Wow. I'm so amazed. She must have taken a long time to build."

"Two and a half years. But we spent another winter putting in the diesel engine, and adding the dolphin nose, so, I suppose we've spent three years on her altogether."

"She's remarkable, Alfred. And you've been all around the world in her."

"Yup."

"Wow. When do you suppose we can go on a voyage?"

"As soon as we can restock and refuel."

"But what about modifying the engine to burn vegetable fat? Should we do that before or after the voyage? Perhaps it would be best to do it first, so we can work out the kinks at sea."

I suddenly had images of us at sea, blowing clouds of blue smoke into the sky, the engine clogged and breaking down. Then we'd spend two weeks pedalling the sub back to shore. Once again I realized the wisdom of Ziegfried's cautionary mind.

"Neither."

"Neither? You don't want to burn vegetable fat?"

"I do, but I called Ziegfried, and asked, and he said no, not until we return to Newfoundland."

"But it's your submarine."

"Yes, but he has the final say on all matters of safety, and he has the right to say when she's fit to sail or not, or if I can make a technical change or not. And he said no. So it's out of my hands."

"Oh, well, if it's out of your hands . . ."

"Yup." And I was glad that it was.

Chapter Nineteen

RESTOCKING THE SUB was unexpectedly fun. Merwin asked me to make a list of the sorts of things we could take with us, which I did, and then we climbed into the camper and went looking for them. His only request was that everything be organic, if possible. That was fine with me.

Our first stop was at an organic farm. Four young girls in dresses and messy hair greeted us when we drove into the yard. They were excited to see Merwin, and made a fuss over Hollie, taking turns carrying him around like a doll. The youngest got him last, and wore a pouty face until she did. Merwin took a large metal bucket out of the back of the camper, and the girls filled it from a larger bucket, using a ladle. The milk had come from the cow that morning, unpasteurized.

"Try it," said Merwin, as he passed me a small cup.

I dipped the cup into the bucket and took a drink. Wow! It was warm, creamy, and incredibly tasty. I didn't know how much we could fit in the sub, but Merwin made such a sour face when I suggested powdered milk that I let him decide.

We also picked up yogurt and goat cheese. Once again, I explained that we had limited space, but Merwin insisted we could freeze the milk and cheese. Okay, but it's a small freezer, I warned. Then, when I pulled money out of my pocket to help pay, Merwin said, no, don't worry about it, he had traded for it already by making an iron railing for their porch. Cool.

Next, we drove to an organic fruit and vegetable market. It was downtown in an old warehouse. The ceiling was made from the timbers of wooden sailing ships, and the floor was made of brick. When we opened the door, I heard someone playing a guitar. Birds flew in and out of the windows, and the air smelled of herbs and flowers, just like Sheba's kitchen.

Everyone knew Merwin. When I tried to pay for the groceries, he told me to put my money away. "No worries," he said. "I rebuilt the windows here. There's no need to pay."

I put my money back in my pocket. "Do you *ever* pay for groceries?"

"Not too often."

At the market we picked up apples, oranges, bananas,

pears, kiwi, avocados, pineapple, lemons, melons, papaya, mangoes, potatoes, yams, carrots, broccoli, onions, squash, and an assortment of fresh herbs. As excited as I was at the sight of all this fresh food, I knew we didn't have room for it. But Merwin insisted we could squeeze it in if we were determined enough. I should have listened to my own experience, but it was hard not to get caught up in his enthusiasm. I wondered if anyone at the market might recognize Hollie and me, but no one seemed to. Merwin, on the other hand, was treated like a celebrity.

After the market, we stopped at an organic bakery. You could smell fresh bread out in the street. Stepping inside was like walking into someone's kitchen. Loaves of bread lined shelves from the floor to the ceiling. I said we had room for maybe three or four. Merwin bought ten. We can freeze them, he said. How, I said, when our freezer will be full of milk and cheese?

The one item Merwin wasn't happy purchasing was diesel fuel. And we needed a lot. This time, I made the purchase. Merwin would never trade anything for a fossil fuel. But fortunately he did bring me to a fuel depot that serviced farmers, and I was permitted to buy at a farmer's rate, which was just a fraction of the regular rate, so I saved hundreds of dollars. We filled six large metal containers, plus my portable surplus tank. But Merwin wore a frown as we carried the fuel back to his house.

We refuelled the sub first. The containers were extremely heavy, and it took both of us to lift them inside the sub, and pour them into the tank. Merwin wore a long face the entire time, but I assured him he'd be happy at sea knowing we'd have all the fuel we needed. I also thought he'd be impressed to see what a clean burning engine actually sounded and felt like, but didn't tell him that yet. He'd see it for himself.

Once the fuel was in, we let the sub air out for a few hours before bringing in the foodstuffs. We didn't want the flavour of diesel to soak into the bread and fruit. The lowering of fresh food into the portal pleased Merwin immensely, and brought back his cheery disposition.

"This is so great, Alfred," he kept saying. "I have always wanted to go to sea in a submarine. I can't believe it is finally happening."

I hoped he would have the experience he was looking for, and that Murphy's Law—if anything can go wrong, it will— would pass us by this time.

Once the sub was refuelled and restocked, we sat down to discuss our route. I suggested hugging the coast all the way around Tasmania. That would be a thousand miles or so, depending upon how many bays and coves we entered, and would take ten days at most, at a relaxing pace. That would be lots of time to teach Merwin how to sail the sub. And we could stop every day to walk on the beach, and pitch our tent every night. Hollie would love it.

"But I want to go to *sea*, Alfred," he complained. "I don't want to stay close to shore. I want to sail as far from land as possible, and feel what's it's like to be out in the deep sea. Why don't we sail to the Southern Ocean?"

"No way!"

"It's not that far."

"It's due south. Every mile south is a mile colder and a mile more dangerous. If you fall overboard in Antarctic waters you'll be dead in four minutes."

"But we won't fall overboard."

"You can't know that."

Merwin looked at me curiously. "I must admit, I'm kind of surprised, Alfred. I would have thought that sailing around the world would have made you more adventurous. No offense, but you sound awfully cautious, like an older person might. Where's your adventurous spirit? Look at the crew of the *Steve Irwin* going down there and risking their lives."

"Yes, but they're sailing on a ship, and are equipped with lifeboats and survival suits. We're not. The risk is too great."

"Bah! How can you be an active environmentalist without taking risks?"

Merwin was challenging me now, and I knew that if I were going to be his captain, I had to act like it. It was my decision where and when we sailed, and his duty to obey that decision, like it or not. I took a deep breath, and answered calmly. "We'll sail around the coast of Tasmania. Don't worry, I guarantee you'll sail in deep water, and feel far from land."

He scrunched up his face, and I could tell that he was biting his tongue. He reminded me a little of my grandfather, and a little of one of the girls at the farm—the fussy one, with the pouty face.

Chapter Twenty

MERWIN TOOK FRITZI to a friend, locked up his house, shop, and boathouse, and we climbed into the sub. We motored out to the centre of the river, submerged, shut everything off, and let the current drag us out to sea like a dead tree. We were undetectable by radar, and pretty near invisible by sonar, unless someone knew exactly where to look, or could hear us; but they couldn't hear us when we weren't making any sound. I told Merwin to find a spot in the bow with Hollie and Seaweed, and sit silently until we had reached the river mouth. Even talking loudly could be heard by a sensitive sonar device, although I was pretty sure the river made too much sound and movement of its own to allow sonar waves to travel undisturbed.

Obediently, Merwin took a seat on the floor beside Hollie, and patted his head. We went down the river at four knots, which took over two hours, roughly the same amount of time we had spent picking snails off the road.

Through the periscope I followed the city lights, and steered carefully beneath the two bridges. There were other vessels in the water, but none approached us, and I doubted anyone ever knew we were there. Once we reached the river's mouth, the lights became fewer and further between, and the seafloor fell sharply. I couldn't believe we were already returning to sea; we had seen so little of Tasmania.

We headed south through Storm Bay to Bruny Island, a rocky island with cliffs I could have sworn were in Newfoundland. At the very bottom of the island was a collection of jagged rocks called the Friars, where the currents were treacherous. We could feel them tugging at us as we passed through. Around the corner was Cloudy Bay, a large horseshoe bay with calm water and sandy beaches, and a place I figured we could pitch our tent, take long walks, and practise diving and surfacing the sub. The whole area was a conservation zone, and was uninhabited. In fact, the whole southwest corner of Tasmania was pretty much one large conservation area.

It was crowded in the sub to say the least. There were bananas, bread, oranges, mangos, and avocados dangling from the rafters, and they bumped against my head whenever I moved. It was worse once Merwin got off the floor. At least he wasn't tall, and didn't have to bend his head. But he was round at the middle, and we couldn't fit in front of the periscope, or in the stern, or anywhere really, at the same time. If he wanted to pass to go towards the bow or stern, I had to press myself against the wall to let him by. At first it was very awkward, but after a while we got the hang of it. It just took a little patience. Now that we had cleared the harbour, and he was free to talk, his first question took me by surprise.

"Alfred?"

"Yes?"

"Where do I go to the bathroom?"

"You have to go to the bathroom?"

"Yes."

"Oh. Well, you have two choices: you can climb the portal, and go over the side; or, you can go in the bucket, which is what you have to do when we're submerged, or in bad weather. I'll show you where it is." I led him to the other side of the ladder, and a small recessed space in the wall by the floor, where I kept the bucket. "It has a lid, and you have to always make sure that it is sealed tightly. When you're done, you put the bucket back in its spot, and pull this flap down to keep it in place, okay? But don't forget to make sure it is sealed and locked in place."

"Okay." He looked around. "Is this all there is?"

"Yes."

"Okay."

"If you tell me when you have to go, I'll make sure to look the other way."

"I have to go now."

"Oh." I turned around.

"Alfred?"

"Yes?"

"What if I get sick?"

"Are you sick?"

"No, but what if I get sick, do I throw up in the same bucket?"

"Yes. That's the only one."

"Oh. I hope I don't get sick."

"Me, too. You should always clean the bucket as soon as you use it . . . I mean, as soon as we are on the surface."

"How do I clean it?"

"You tie it to this rope, climb the portal, open the hatch, and throw it into the sea. It's a good idea to drag it through the water for a few minutes. The salt water helps keep it clean. And that reminds me to tell you about the most important rule on the sub."

"What's that?"

"Before you ever climb out of the portal, you must always strap on the harness that's hanging there. That's the unbreakable rule, and believe me, it's important. Why don't you go and practise doing that now? I'll surface the sub."

"Can I use the bucket first?"

"Oh, yah. Sorry."

"That's okay."

There was only one harness. But I had lots of rope, so, while Merwin was using the bucket, I fashioned a makeshift harness out of rope. Then I secured it to a ten-foot length of rope, and that was the harness I would use.

Five miles offshore, we surfaced before the sun had broken the horizon. I showed Merwin how to wear the harness, and he climbed out of the portal with the sealed bucket in one hand. I followed him, wearing the other harness, and Seaweed followed me, then turned around and went back inside. It was still too dark for him to see the shore, and the wind was gusting. Merwin looked up at the dark sky. It was filled with stars. His face was lit with wonder.

"This is truly awesome."

I nodded. "It's one of the great things about travelling in a sub—you see the most amazing skies. Be careful when you open the bucket."

"Okay."

"And make sure to hold on to a handle with one hand when you swing it. It's easier than you think to fall in the sea."

"Okay. This is so great, Alfred. I'm so happy to be here."

"I'm glad." I watched as he leaned over and grabbed a handle on the portal. He put the bucket down by his feet and tried to open the lid with his other hand. It looked awkward. He should have opened the lid first. Then, when he stood up, he lost his balance as a rogue wave rocked the sub. He attempted to throw the bucket anyway, tossing it into the wind, but it was quickly flung back at him, hitting him on the shoulder and knocking his grip free from the handle. I ducked as the bucket bounced through the air. Merwin made a desperate grab for it, missed, and went flying over the side with a big splash.

I didn't jump in after him. I knew he was wearing the harness, and I wanted to see how well he would handle the situation. He had claimed to be a good swimmer.

"Whoa!" he yelled. "It's cold!"

"I bet."

"How do you climb up this thing?"

"There are handles on the side."

"I can't see them. It's too dark!"

"Feel for them."

I waited. I could hear him splashing around. Eventually, he found them, and slowly pulled himself up.

"Well . . . that was refreshing." He handed me the bucket. "I think it's clean now."

Protected from the open sea, Cloudy Bay was calm and shallow, with a sandy floor in places, which was perfect for teaching Merwin how to dive and surface. The beach was sandy, too, and long and wide, which was great for Hollie. As much as he enjoyed tramping around in cities, his favourite place to run was on a sandy beach. On top of that, the bay was secluded. There was not a soul in sight.

Normally at a beach I'd drop anchor, inflate the rubber dinghy, and paddle to shore. But halfway around the bay was a natural breakwater that jutted out about fifty feet or so, and the water there was thirty feet deep, so we tied up, climbed out, and walked over the rocks to the sand. We never bothered to shut the hatch because there were no waves, rain, or people around. I was happy to let the sub air out anyway. It smelled stronger with two people in it.

Hollie hit the sand running, and grabbed the first stick he saw. Seaweed took off in search of crabs, and Merwin and I strolled down the beach. On the way, I ate two of the bananas and three of the oranges that had been bumping against my head. Merwin ate some kiwi and a mango. He was feeling deeply inspired. His eyes were all glossy and happy.

"Alfred?"

"Yes?"

"This is a great life."

"Yes, it is."

Chapter Twenty-one

I WAS WOKEN BY RADAR. Two days had passed since we left Cloudy Bay for the open sea, although each day we returned to shore to spend a few hours on the beach. Merwin complained that we weren't sailing to deeper water, but I wasn't going to deny Hollie his runs on the beach.

The first night we had slept on shore, but the second night we were out of sight of land, and went to sleep with the hatch wide open, beneath a starry sky. We were also outside of the busy shipping lane, so I wasn't worried about being struck by another vessel in the middle of the night. I trusted myself to hear the radar if it beeped.

I saw the faint reflection of light bounce off the wall like a puff of green smoke. Everyone on the sub was sleeping. Hollie was curled up on his blanket. Running on the beach for hours each day had worn him out. Seaweed sat as still as a stone. Lights and sounds meant nothing to him if they were not accompanied by the sight or smell of food. Merwin was sprawled on the floor of the bow on his sleeping bag. One of his legs was dangling ungracefully in the pocket of the observation window, his head was lying crooked, his mouth was gaping open, and he was snoring like a buffalo.

I raised my head. Probably it was a freighter coming wide around the shipping lane, but still heading towards Hobart. That it wasn't in the normal shipping route didn't concern me; captains will change course for any number of reasons. What did concern me was the possibility that she was a naval vessel, or coast guard. Did she know we were here, or was it just a coincidence? Well, she knew we were here *now*, of course, just as we knew she was there. I slipped out of bed. I figured I'd better see which way she was heading exactly. I didn't want to get run over by a freighter in the middle of the night.

Moving through the dark, I tilted my head to avoid hitting a bag of oranges, and got struck in the eye by the end of a banana. "Ouch!" Merwin must have moved things around on his way to bed. My cry woke him up.

"What's up?"

I found the radar screen, rubbed my eye, and took a glance.

"There's another vessel in the water. It's probably nothing. Did you move the bananas?"

"Yeah. Sorry. I was hungry."

I stared at the screen. The vessel was eight miles west. She was not coming our way. Merwin got to his feet and came over. He looked excited. "What is it?"

"It's nothing. She's not coming our way. We can go back to bed."

"Where is she going?"

I looked at the screen again. "South."

"Due south?"

"Yes. Looks like it."

"So she's going to the Antarctic then?"

"I don't know. Maybe."

"There's nowhere else to go if you're heading south."

"I suppose so." I was ready to go back to bed.

"She must be another tanker, Alfred. She's going to refuel the whaling ships."

"What? No way. You can't know that."

"She must be, Alfred. Who else would be heading there?"

"*Lots* of ships: research vessels, icebreakers, the coast guard . . ."

Merwin shook his head. "Not now. Not right now. I know because I follow the marine news. There's nobody heading to the Antarctic now. It must be another tanker that's sneaking down there, hoping nobody will see her. We should go after her, Alfred."

I shook my head. "No way. We probably couldn't even catch her, and she's probably not a tanker anyway."

"But what if she is, Alfred?"

I shrugged. "There's nothing we can do about it anyway."

"Maybe there is, though." Man, Merwin was determined.

"How? What could we possibly do?"

"I don't know. But we won't find out unless we try."

"It's crazy."

"Maybe it's crazy, but the Sea Shepherd Society is down there. And they're saving whales. Maybe you have to be a little crazy to do that, but they're doing it."

I stared at the screen and sighed. The vessel was moving steadily, not fast. Maybe we could catch up to her, I wasn't sure. It would take hours to find out. And all of that time, we'd be heading due south, which was exactly what Merwin wanted in the first place.

"What have we got to lose? What are we doing that's so important we can't follow her to see what she's up to?"

He was right again. "Okay. We'll try to get close enough to see what kind of vessel she is."

"She's a tanker. I can feel it in my gut."

The moment we started our engine and began to chase the unknown vessel, she knew we were coming. She would know that because she'd see a little blinking dot on her radar that was now following her, very slowly getting closer. And that little dot was us.

If I were her, and saw another vessel coming after us, I'd

change my course, and watch to see if my chaser changed course. That's what I would expect this vessel to do, too, if she were a naval ship, or coast guard. But she never altered her course, nor her speed. Her behaviour was what you'd expect of a tanker, in fact—slow, steady, and unchanging. Tankers pick up speed and slow down very gradually. They don't like to turn, and do it with great difficulty. I pointed these things out to Merwin just for his instruction. He didn't need any convincing that she was a tanker.

But we were gaining on her at a painfully slow rate. After five hours at our top speed of twenty-one knots, we were still five miles behind, and couldn't spot her through the binoculars yet, which was another indication she might be a tanker—heavy with oil and riding low in the water.

Another five hours later, I heard Merwin holler from the portal, where he had been leaning against the open hatch for hours, with the cold wind blowing in his face. "I see her! I see her! There she is!"

I went to the bottom of the ladder and looked up. "Let me see."

Merwin climbed out to make room for me to come up. He was wearing the harness. I was surprised to feel how cold the air had become. We had been sailing south for ten hours, which meant we had come over two hundred miles closer to the Antarctic. Merwin's face was pink with windburn, and his lips were blue. It was time for him to come inside. He handed me the binoculars, and I took a glance. As I scanned the line of the horizon I saw a bump. Focussing carefully, I could just make out the fat bridge of a tanker. Merwin's gut feeling had been correct. I nodded my head. "Yup. There she is. Looks like a tanker to me."

"I told you!"

"You were right."

"It had to be. She's on her way to refuel the whalers. We've got to stop her, Alfred."

"Stop her? What are you talking about? We can't stop her. That would be like an ant trying to stop an elephant."

"Think of David and Goliath."

"Okay, but we don't have a slingshot that would put a dent in that hull. Besides, she's carrying oil, don't forget. The last thing we'd ever want to do is cause her to have an accident."

"I know. That's the whole reason tankers are not allowed below the 60-degree latitude line, because the Southern Ocean is a sanctuary, and an oil spill would be catastrophic. So she shouldn't be going there. But that's where she's heading, Alfred. She's going where she's not allowed to go. Don't you think that gives us the right to try and stop her?"

"I suppose so, but how?"

"I don't know, but I don't want to give up before we even try."

We stood and stared at the horizon, where, without binoculars, the tanker was just a speck among ribbons of water. The sea was growing rougher. It was cold, and it looked ugly. I turned towards Merwin. He was shivering.

"Time to get inside and warm up," I said.

"Nah, I'm good."

No, he wasn't. "Inside," I said with a friendly tone. "Captain's orders."

He started to raise the binoculars. "I'm just going to . . ."

I grabbed his arm. He turned and looked at me with surprise.

"Get inside," I said firmly. "That's an order." I reached my hand for the binoculars. He passed them to me and dropped his head.

"I'm sorry. Okay, I'll get inside."

I moved out of the way to let him climb in. Thank Heavens he did; I didn't know what I would have done if he hadn't.

Chapter Twenty-two

EVERY MILE SOUTH REALLY was a mile colder and more dangerous, and the change came quickly sailing near top speed, and not stopping, because the tanker never stopped. If we let her go out of radar range, we'd never find her again.

That meant we had to take turns sleeping, and keeping an eye on the ship. I decided to take first watch, and let Merwin sleep. Fortunately I didn't have to argue with him about it because he fell asleep during supper. He was drinking soup out of a metal bowl, and crunching four-day-old bread when I heard the bowl rattle against the observation window. He must have been deeply exhausted because he fell asleep in the middle of a sentence, too. I put his pillow under his head, lifted his sleeping bag over him, and checked to see that his mouth was free of bread. That was easy to do because he slept with his mouth wide open. If he slept like that in the woods, he must have swallowed a lot of flies.

Over the next ten hours, with the current behind us, we travelled almost two hundred miles, and narrowed the distance between the tanker and us to two miles. She wasn't very big, as tankers go, but was carrying plenty of oil to refuel the Japanese whaling fleet. The sun went down, and then, just a couple of hours later, it came right back up. As at the North Pole, the South Pole had twenty-four hours of sunlight on a summer's day, and twenty-four hours of darkness on a winter's day. We were still outside the Antarctic Circle, but close enough to experience short nights, and very cold air and water. I wondered if we would run into growlers, those treacherous chunks of ice that break off from icebergs and float just beneath the surface, invisible and deadly. We had hit several of them in the Arctic, and although the sub was designed to bounce when it struck something, rather than dent or crack, we all received bruises from being thrown around inside. I banged my mouth against the periscope one time, and put my teeth through my lip.

But we hadn't sailed far enough south yet to run into growlers. We came upon something else though, or, I should say, it came upon us. It was travelling beside us and I didn't even know it.

I was leaning against the hatch, watching the moon and stars, when there was a blast of air, and ocean spray in my face. I knew right away what it was. When the sun came up and turned the sea into a blazing carpet of orange, I saw a large blue whale swimming along beside us. Then I noticed that there were two: mother and baby. The baby was almost twice the size of the sub, so it wasn't a newborn. The mother was twice as big as that.

They swam beside us for hours. They'd disappear for a while, and then come back. When the sun rose higher, I saw them up close, because they swam so near I could almost have reached over and touched them. I saw their eyes, and they saw me, and I knew that they were saying hello. I could feel it. So I said hello back. Then I brought Hollie out. He had seen whales before, and was fascinated by them, but I think the whales were even more fascinated by him. They stared at him with such intensity. And when he barked, the mother whale slapped her tail on the water. If that wasn't a greeting, I didn't know what was.

A few hours later, I was inside making tea when I heard Merwin stirring in the bow.

"What time is it?"

"Seven o'clock."

"How long have I been sleeping?"

"About ten hours."

"Wow, why didn't you wake me?"

"There was no need to. Besides, you needed the sleep."

"It's so quiet and warm in here it's easy to sleep."

"I know. Do you want tea?"

"I'd kill for tea. Do you want me to make French toast?"

"That would be great. We have company."

"We do? Who?"

"They're outside."

"They are? Who's outside? Another ship?"

"Go take a look."

Merwin wiped the sleep from his eyes, climbed the portal, and strapped on the harness. A few seconds later I heard him yell. "*Whales!* Oh, fantastic!"

Later, when we sat down for breakfast, Merwin spoke excitedly about the whales, and about Captain Watson. Whales were Merwin's favourite animal, and the captain was his hero. "I believe that whales are the smartest and kindest creatures on the planet," he said. "They're way smarter than we are, and much kinder. They know that we kill them, and yet they still like us. It's as if they're waiting for us to grow up, to stop killing, and to live in peace."

"Have you ever met Captain Watson?"

"Like you, I've seen him up close, but have never spoken with him. He's a busy man, and doesn't stay long in one place. There are many countries where he cannot go, or he'll be thrown into jail. Especially in Japan, where they'd lock him up and probably throw away the key. They must really hate him there. He has devoted his whole life to saving whales and dolphins, and that has made him the number one enemy of the Japanese whaling industry. But he's doing what nobody else has the guts to do. I admire him tremendously."

Merwin kept talking, but I had gone for such a long time without sleep that it was getting hard to hold my head up. His voice started sounding like a radio in another room. With a belly full of French toast, I plopped down on my cot, and shut my eyes. I was asleep in seconds.

Merwin was under strict orders to wake me if there were any problems, or if he wasn't sure what to do. The sub was cruising along at nearly top speed, and the engine was purring like a cat. I checked it before lying down just to make sure it wasn't straining. Merwin was so impressed with the engine that he just stared at it and didn't know what to say. I was very proud of it. All he had to do while I slept was watch the radar, keep an eye on the tanker, and make sure we didn't get too close. He said, no problem, it was a piece of cake. I thanked him for a wonderful breakfast, and went to bed.

I fell into a deep sleep, and had strange dreams. That always happened when I ate too much. In one of my dreams there was a monster ahead of us. Merwin was there, too. We were travelling through a jungle, and we could hear the monster roar, but couldn't see it, even though it was right in front of us. I kept trying to warn Merwin to watch out for it, but he was flipping French toast and whistling at Hollie. I woke from the dream in a half-wake state, and wasn't sure where I was or what was going on. I could still hear the monster rumbling, even as I opened my eyes. How could that be when I was awake?

Suddenly, in a panic, I recognized the sound I was hearing,

and knew where it was coming from. I sprang out of bed, and flew up the portal. There, in front of us, not more than seventy-five feet, was the stern of the tanker rising out of the water like an iron giant. She had cut her engines, and we were about to crash into her. How could this have happened? Where was Merwin?

I raced back inside and shut the engine. Then I pulled the wheel and swung to port as sharply as possible. The sub lost speed as it turned, but we couldn't avoid striking the hull of the tanker lightly. It was just a bump, and did no damage to anyone, yet it made a lot of noise inside the sub. I saw Merwin's head pop up from inside the stern, just before we hit.

"What's up?" he said, when he saw me turn the wheel.

"Brace yourself!" I yelled, but we struck the hull before he had a chance to, and the collision knocked him off his feet. "What did we hit?" he called from the floor.

"The tanker."

"*What*? How is that possible?"

I started the engine again, and headed away from the ship. I wanted to put distance between us as quickly as possible in case there were men with rifles on her deck. It had happened before. Merwin climbed the portal to look for himself, and then came back inside. "How is it possible?" he asked again.

"I don't know. I guess she cut her speed. When was the last time you checked on her?"

"About an hour ago, I guess. Or maybe two. We were gaining on her so slowly. She was still pretty far ahead last time I looked. I don't know how we could have caught her so fast."

"What were you doing?"

"Peeling potatoes in the cold room. And then I got distracted. Look."

He showed me a handful of small sculptures—two whales and a submarine. He had sculpted them out of potatoes.

Chapter Twenty-three

WE NEVER KNEW WHY the tanker cut her speed and slowed to a crawl. No one from the ship tried to communicate with us, and we didn't try to communicate with her. Had she suddenly realized she was being followed by a submarine, and thought we were a lot bigger and more dangerous than we were? Or did she maybe not even know we were here? But she had to know, because she would have seen us on radar. Was it because she knew she was heading for the 60-degree latitude line, beyond which she wasn't legally allowed to go? Did she think we were a naval vessel perhaps, and were watching to see if she would cross that line, and waiting to arrest her captain and crew if she did? We had no way of knowing, but that seemed the most likely reason, and it appeared to be confirmed by the fact that she picked up speed again once she saw how tiny we were, and that we were not contesting her in any way. Merwin wanted to. He wanted to fire flares across her bow, but I said no. It wouldn't mean anything to her, and would be a waste of valuable flares.

So, we watched and listened as she revved up her enormous engines, churned up the water in her wake, and very slowly began to pick up speed. Dropping back half a mile, just enough to avoid the heaviest turbulence, we followed as before.

A few hours later, the whales came back. I was surprised. For some reason they had attached themselves to us—perhaps because they liked Hollie, or were curious about him. Or maybe it was because Merwin started singing to them. Merwin said it was because they knew that we loved them. That was something Sheba would have said. Merwin believed that whales were so advanced they could know what our intentions were even without us expressing them. On some level, they just knew, as if they were reading our minds. That sounded pretty unbelievable to me, though I wanted to believe it, especially when I watched them, or looked into their eyes. But I remembered Ziegfried's warning to me to remain objective and scientific about things, and not let my emotions tell me what was happening; otherwise I would go through life believing that butterflies were happy, and frogs were bored. While that seemed like important advice, I had to confess that Merwin's view was a lot more convincing when we were actually in the presence of the whales.

There was nothing but water between us and the 60th latitude line, but it was still a thousand miles away, which was at least two more days of non-stop sailing, if the current stayed with us. It seemed crazy to me to travel so far south so unprepared. We only had one winter parka—mine—and one wet suit—also mine. We had a rubberized dinghy and an inflatable kayak—neither designed for cold weather, let alone Antarctic conditions. We did have plenty of diesel fuel, not vegetable fat, thanks to Ziegfried's cautious wisdom, and a supply of food to last us two weeks, or maybe three, although the fresh fruit would be gone by the end of the first week, and the bread was already drying out. Fortunately it still tasted good in hot stew.

But I, too, couldn't help wanting to follow the tanker now, and I hoped that somehow we might prevent her from refuelling the whalers, though I couldn't see how. That we were being accompanied by whales made it seem all the more justified. It felt as though they had come to guide us down to where help was most needed. Merwin was absolutely convinced of that.

Over the next two days, the whales continued to swim alongside us, and we became very attached to them. It was hard not to. They were beautiful and they were gentle. The baby behaved just like a human baby would, tugging at its mother, and wanting to play all the time. The mother seemed sometimes joyful, and sometimes just tired. I dug out my camera, and took lots of pictures of both of them coming right to the hull of the sub, with Merwin leaning over in the harness, singing to them, and touching them.

Then, on the second day, Merwin had a special request. We were sitting down with bowls of stew and crusty bread, when he came out with it. "I have always dreamed of swimming with whales."

I nodded my head. "Cool."

"It's one of my life's dreams actually."

I nodded again. "I think it would be awesome."

"I'm glad you think so. I'd like to swim with these ones."

"What? No way! It's too cold here. You'd freeze to death."

"But you've got a wet suit."

"Yes, but, no offence, it wouldn't fit you. And even if you *could* get into it, the water is still life-threateningly cold."

"Cold water doesn't bother me. I'm from Tasmania."

"I'm from Newfoundland, and I can tell you that this water will kill you." I looked at him to see if he was really being serious. He was. He was nuts. "I don't think you realize how cold the water really is, Merwin."

"I think I do. I'm only talking about going in for a couple of minutes, nothing longer than that."

"I'm sorry, but it's a crazy idea. I can't allow it."

Surprisingly, he didn't make a face, as I thought he would, and he never complained. We continued to eat in silence.

After that, it was his turn to catch some sleep. I dimmed the lights once he got comfortable in his sleeping bag. If he were feeling sour at me, he certainly didn't show it. I should have guessed that it was only because he hadn't dropped the idea. He went to bed scheming to find another way. I had to give him credit—he never gave up until he got what he wanted.

During the night, I listened to the sounds the whales were making: clicking noises, grunts, and song-like whistles. They were mysterious sounds. There was something childlike about them, and something ancient. Whales were the caretakers of the sea, keeping an eye on it for millions of years. It amazed me to think how enormous they were yet they caused no destruction. They were as gentle and delicate as deer. As I leaned against the hatch with Hollie in my arms, and we listened to their voices, I had to agree with Merwin that they were more advanced than we were. I could better understand now why Captain Watson would devote his whole life to saving them. If we couldn't save the whales, what hope was there for the rest of the world?

After the long night—the actual darkness of which lasted barely an hour—I was tired and ready for bed. I woke Merwin with a cup of coffee, and told him once again to keep an eye on things, and this time to make a visual check either through the periscope, or the portal, every fifteen minutes without fail. With a nod of his head he agreed. Then he asked me if he could try on my wet suit while I was sleeping. He just wanted to know if it would fit. What if there was an emergency, he said, and he had to wear it? He said he solemnly promised not to climb out of the portal with it. I shrugged my shoulders and said okay, but didn't think he'd be able to get into it. It was hard enough for me to get into it. I pulled it out from underneath my mattress, tossed it to him, and went to bed.

"You promise you won't go outside with it?" I said, as I rolled over on my side.

"I promise."

"Okay then. Good luck." Boy, was he going to need it.

Chapter Twenty-four

ONLY A FEW HOURS AFTER I went to bed, I felt a tugging at my shoulder.

"Alfred?"

"Yes?"

"Sorry to bother you."

"That's okay. Is everything all right?"

"Yeah, everything's great. Listen, I'm going to buy you a new wet suit when we get back to Tasmania, okay?"

"You're going to buy me a new wet suit? Why?"

"Because I have to cut this one."

"You have to cut it? Why?"

"Because I can't get it off. I've tried for hours. I'm going crazy, and my hands and feet are turning numb. Would you help me cut it off?"

I sat up. Merwin looked terrible. His face was as red as a strawberry. He was drenched in sweat, and his face, hands, and feet were swollen. I didn't know how he had managed to squeeze into the suit, but the zipper that ran the length of his back was coming apart. His belly stuck out smooth, round and black, like a big bowling ball.

"Yah, we'd better cut it off. Let me get my jackknife. Did you try wetting it?"

"Wetting it?"

"Yah, it's designed to stretch when it's wet."

He looked down at himself. "No, I never thought of that. Maybe we should try that first."

"Okay." I climbed the portal with a pot, dipped it into the sea, and came back inside. "It's going to be really cold."

"I sure hope so. I'm burning up."

I poured the water over his shoulders and down his neck.

"*Whoa!* That *is* cold."

"Sorry."

"No, it's okay. Hey, I feel it loosening up already."

"Yah, it should. If you jumped in the sea, it would loosen up completely, and you'd feel free and comfortable, well, except for freezing to death."

"Really?"

"Yes, but you'd be overcome with the cold."

"I don't think I would be right now, actually. Why don't we try it, now that I've gone to all the trouble to get the darn thing on? I can put the harness over it, and go out on the rope, and then come right back in. And if I have any trouble, you can simply pull me over with the rope."

I remembered the day I fell into the sea, and was about to say no when I looked into his eyes, saw his frustration and passion, and thought it over. If I were as hot as he was right now, I'd want to jump into the sea, too. And it was true that I could pull him back to the sub if he couldn't make it himself. It seemed an unnecessary risk really, and yet, on the other hand, it was one of his life's dreams. How could I deny him that?

"Yah, okay."

"Really? You agree?"

"Sure. Why not? Believe me though, you're in for a shock."

"I don't mind. That's awesome. Thanks, Captain."

I smiled. "You're welcome."

And so, Merwin went swimming with the whales after all. I helped him up the ladder, out of the portal, and down onto the hull. The wet suit was so tight he could barely move his arms and legs. I wore my parka because the wind was strong and cold. I suggested he lower himself a little at a time, but he had no patience left, and said he'd rather deal with the shock all at once. I held onto the rope and kept it away from the propeller as he half-jumped half-fell into the water. He hollered and thrashed around for a while, as the water pulled him to the end of a seventy-five-foot rope, and then dragged him behind the sub like a rubber dinghy. He knew that the more he thrashed about, the sooner his body's heat would warm up the suit. It wouldn't actually make him comfortable, but might take the sting out of the cold for a few minutes. We had agreed that when he was ready to come back inside, he would raise his arm into the air, and I would pull him in. If he didn't raise it after ten minutes, I would begin pulling on the rope anyway. In truth, I expected to see his arm go up long before ten minutes were up.

But it didn't.

The whales were curious to see Merwin splashing about in the water behind the sub, and swam closer. They looked closely at his face, to check and see if he was the same man who had sung to them. When they saw that he was, they slapped their tails on the water. The mother did it first, and then the baby. They recognized him.

For ten full minutes Merwin dangled at the end of the rope like a fishing bobber. He wasn't actually swimming; he was more like slowly water-skiing on his belly. We didn't shut off the engine because we didn't want to fall behind the tanker. But we did slow down a little, so our wake wouldn't be so turbulent. I watched as Merwin ducked his head beneath the waves several times, trying to see the whales under water. He also tried to manoeuvre closer to the mother, but the force of the water was too strong. He was having a good time though. I could hear him yelling with excitement. I carried out my camera and took pictures.

At ten minutes exactly, I started reeling him in. He waved

frantically for me to stop, but I wouldn't. I knew what the danger was. He was so passionate and stubborn he didn't care about the dangers of hypothermia, and was willing to risk everything just to swim with the whales. It took almost five minutes to pull him to the boat and help him out of the water. He had more freedom of movement now that the suit was soaked through, but was exhausted, more exhausted than I had realized when. he went in the water. He had used up so much energy just getting into the suit.

It was hard work getting him up the portal and down the ladder. But he was very happy. He kept saying, "What a thrill!" but was almost delirious with cold and fatigue. Once we were inside, it wasn't necessary to cut the wet suit. It peeled off him like a banana skin. But once he was free, I discovered that he was shivering badly. His lips were trembling.

"I'll make you some hot chocolate," I said. "That'll warm you up."

"Thank you, Alfred. I mean, thank you, Captain. That would be amazing."

I helped him to his sleeping bag, then put the last of our fresh milk into a pot and started to heat it up. There was nothing as wonderful as hot chocolate in cold seas. But when I brought the cup over to him, I found him fast asleep already, and he would sleep for the next twelve hours straight. So I drank the hot chocolate myself.

I was tired, too, but had to stay awake to follow the tanker. Having stopped once, she might again, and I couldn't risk striking her hull at full speed. So, I spent a few hours riding the bike, playing with Hollie, and reading. I started the book by Thoreau again, but this time was able to pay attention, and discovered that what Margaret had said was true: Thoreau and I thought a lot alike. I mean, I agreed with everything he wrote. I couldn't believe he was writing from a hundred and fifty years ago, because it seemed like what he was saying was true today, even though it sounded old-fashioned. *Walden* quickly became my favourite book

Twelve hours after Merwin went to sleep, I brought him a cup of coffee and woke him up. He was groggy and dizzy but it was time to trade off again. He would be on watch, and I would get some sleep. He was beginning to see how being at sea, even in the comfort of a submarine, could be very tiring. In truth, I found it easier to be alone. I was getting only half as much sleep as I was used to. But in spite of that, and in spite of being cramped, I realized I was starting to like having him around. I was getting used to him, and learning something important. I couldn't put it into words yet exactly, but I knew it had something to do with saving the planet.

Chapter Twenty-five

ONCE AGAIN, I WAS woken by a tug at my shoulder.

"Sorry to wake you, Captain, but there are a couple of lights flashing on the radar screen that weren't there before, and they look like they're coming this way."

Ever since he swam with the whales, Merwin had taken to calling me captain all the time, and he wasn't joking.

"Thanks for waking me." I climbed out of bed, and shuffled over to the screen. The tanker had crossed the invisible 60th latitude line, and there were two vessels coming to meet her. They were still eight miles away. They must have been whalers planning to rendezvous, to siphon oil from her belly. I wished we had come up with some way to stop that from happening, but we hadn't. Merwin was full of ideas, but none of them was the least bit realistic. I wanted to stop the transfer of oil just as much as he did, but I didn't think he believed me, because I had shot down all of his ideas.

"We could ram her propeller, and break it."

"Way too dangerous. Besides, we don't want to disable her, or prevent her from sailing out of the area."

"We could sail ahead of her, turn around and play chicken with her at night. With lights and flares we could make her think we are much bigger than we are, and frighten her crew into turning around."

"She couldn't turn around quickly, even if she wanted to. We might make her alter her course a little, but she'd figure out it was us soon enough. She knows we've been following her."

"We could ram her sideways, punch a small hole in her that would force her to sail back to Australia as soon as possible."

I had to wonder what Merwin thought we were sailing. If we rammed the tanker at full speed, we would simply bounce off, and probably not even leave a dent. And if we *were* able to put a hole in her hull, she'd leak oil all the way back to Australia. I could tell how passionate Merwin felt about the situation by how crazy his ideas were.

"We have to try *something*, Captain. We didn't come all this way to do nothing."

"I know, but we didn't come down here to commit suicide either, or to cause an environmental disaster. Let's wait until the whalers attempt to pump oil from her; maybe we can do something then."

"Like what?"

"I don't know."

Merwin shook his head. "It'll be too late. We have to do something now."

But there was nothing to do except wait. When the two vessels were five miles away, the tanker cut her engines. She had to; they were coming directly towards her, without veering, which left her little choice. They would have picked us up on radar also, so there was no point in trying to hide, but I decided to submerge to periscope depth anyway, and swing in a wide arc around the tanker so that they wouldn't know exactly where we were. Taking turns at the periscope, Merwin and I stared without blinking as the two vessels sailed into sight, and boy, did we get a surprise!

The first ship wore a large skull and crossbones right across her bridge, and was painted black and blue. It was the *Steve Irwin*! The second ship was called the *Bob Barker*, and was a sister ship. These were not whalers; these were the ships of the Sea Shepherd Society. They had come to prevent the tanker from entering the Southern Ocean. And they were not fooling around. Their sailing manoeuvres left the tanker no option but to shut her engines and drift to a stop.

"Yay!" Merwin and I both shouted.

The *Steve Irwin* and *Bob Barker* parked themselves in front of the tanker's bow like two dogs cornering a bear. Then, they must have had a radio exchange, because the tanker fired up her engines, the ships gave way, and the tanker started moving again, in a very wide arc—it took her more than a mile to make it—and headed back the way she had come, with the ships on either side of her. They were escorting her back above the 60th parallel, and sending her back to Australia. We followed. Merwin was ecstatic.

"Do you see, Captain? Do you see why I admire Captain Watson and his society so much? Other groups work for change; the Sea Shepherd Society *makes* it happen."

I couldn't argue with that. Watching the ships force the tanker around astonished me. I knew we were witnessing something remarkable. The Sea Shepherd Society was not part of any navy, coast guard, or police force; they were just a group of courageous people standing up for the whales, telling the tanker to take her bloody oil and get the heck out of here; these are protected waters. Merwin and I both had tears of joy in our eyes as the tanker turned on her tail, and headed north.

But she didn't go far. And our excitement was soon mixed with suspicion. The Shepherd ships accompanied the tanker across the 60th parallel, turned around, and sailed back south. They had whalers to chase. As the *Steve Irwin* passed about quarter of a mile away, Merwin and I waved and cheered from the hull, and she returned our greeting with a few blasts of her horn. We wanted to let them know we were here, and that we would follow the tanker all the way back to Australia.

But that was not what happened. Once the Shepherd ships

had disappeared from radar, the tanker slowed to a mere five knots. So we did, too. This was very suspicious. What was she doing? Against the current it felt as though we weren't even moving. A few hours later, she made a very gradual turn portside. That was sneaky. Now, she was heading very slightly south of west. Why? There was nowhere to go but Africa, which was unbelievably far away. What was she up to?

We found out about ten hours later, when two lights appeared on the radar screen once again, coming from the Southern Ocean. Had the Shepherd ships discovered that the tanker had stayed in the area, and were coming back to chase her away?

I watched the screen closely, and stared through the periscope. But we were not in range, and I couldn't see anything, so I climbed the portal with the binoculars. It was nighttime now, though not actually dark, just a lingering twilight. Merwin was sleeping. At five miles, I spotted the lights of one of the ships, and then the other. As before, the tanker cut her engines and drifted to a stop. I closed our distance to a quarter of a mile, went back inside, shut off the engine, and watched through the periscope. As darkness fell, I couldn't see the approaching ships, only their lights. From two miles away, they appeared to be the same size as the Shepherd ships. But at half a mile, even in the dark, I could tell that they were whalers. Thirsty for oil, they had come north of the 60th parallel to refuel.

I woke Merwin. He was very groggy. "What is it, Captain?"

"The whalers have come. They're going to refuel. I don't know if there's anything we can do, but I thought you'd like to know."

"I sure would. Thanks for waking me."

"You're welcome."

Once again, we took turns at the periscope. This time, Merwin tried harder to come up with realistic ideas. He knew I wouldn't agree to anything that wasn't, even though I wanted to stop the whalers from refuelling just as much as he did. If they couldn't refuel, they'd have to sail back to Japan, which would mean that more whales would live. We had to try something.

"We simply have to sail between them," Merwin said. "That's what Captain Watson does. I've seen it on TV."

I shook my head. The tanker, although it was a small one, was at least five hundred feet long. Each of the whalers was about half that size, which meant that they were still ten times bigger than we were. If we sailed between them, we'd get crushed. But that didn't seem to concern Merwin at all.

"They'll back off if we do it. They'll get frustrated, and back away."

"In the dark, they won't even see us!" The whalers had chosen to refuel in the dark, probably in the hope that no one would see them from the air.

"We'll use the floodlights. They'll see us then. And we can shoot flares."

I hesitated. I turned and looked at Hollie and Seaweed. I

didn't want to put their lives at risk.

"Captain, when they refuel, they're going to kill whales. You know that. We have to do something."

I felt such a dilemma. I didn't want to risk the lives of my crew, yet wanted to save the whales. There was no easy solution. "Yah, okay. We'll give it a try. But the moment it feels too dangerous to me, we're out of here."

"Aye, aye, Captain. I stand at the ready."

So we motored around the stern of the tanker, and waited until one of the whalers came alongside her. I stayed inside at the controls, and stole quick glances through the periscope. Merwin climbed the portal with the flare gun, and put the harness on. He got ready, on my command, to blast them with light and flares.

The channel of water between the two ships was very narrow, and the movement of the sea uneven. The ships didn't want to bang into each other, but had to be close enough to transfer oil. I watched as they started to pass heavy hoses from one deck to the other, and then I gave the command.

"Lights!"

Through the periscope I saw our floodlights beam across the hulls of the two ships, but they weren't high enough, and wouldn't interfere with anything. All they accomplished was to let them know we were suicidal enough to put ourselves in between two vessels that could easily squash us. Our hull sat at sea level. From their perspective, it must have seemed as though we weren't even here. In fact, the threat we brought to them was not a threat to either ship; it was the threat of causing the deaths of a couple of crazy environmentalists, which would look bad on TV. Merwin explained that both the Japanese and Shepherd ships carried film cameras, and that their skirmishes in the past had often found their way onto TV. As desperate as our action seemed, it had to be taken seriously in a time when environmental issues were always in the news. The Japanese whalers, after all, were catching whales under the pretence of using them for research, which was a lie. If they were seen to act so aggressively as to damage another vessel, and kill people, they surely wouldn't look very scientific. This battle wasn't taking place only at sea, but on television, too.

"What do you call a person who dies for a cause?" I yelled up to Merwin. I knew that there was a word for it but couldn't remember it.

He yelled back. "A martyr."

"Right. Be careful. We're not here to become martyrs."

My heart was racing as we motored about a third of the way between the two ships. Then, I heard the bang of the flare gun. I told Merwin to shoot straight up, and try not to hit anyone. If they wouldn't notice our floodlights, they certainly would see our flares.

And they did, because the next thing we knew, a powerful burst of water pounded down on us, gushed inside the portal, and started to flood the sub. I heard Merwin yell. I shouted as loudly as I could over the noise. "Water cannon! Merwin, get inside! Shut the hatch! Shut the hatch!"

"I can't! The water's too strong!"

Whoever was aiming the water cannon knew exactly what they were doing. They were trying to sink us. The force of the water was so strong it was rocking the sub back and forth. We banged into one ship, then the other. This was insane. I hit the engine switch and cranked it up full blast. We started to move forward between the two ships. The water cannon followed us, but not as accurately as before.

"I've got it!" Merwin yelled as he shut the hatch. I switched from engine power to batteries. As we cleared the bow of the whaler, I hit the dive switch, and we went under.

"Are you all right?" I said, as the sub grew suddenly quiet.

"Yah, I'm okay, Captain."

But he wasn't. When he climbed down the ladder, there was blood all over his face.

Chapter Twenty-six

MERWIN SUFFERED A broken nose when the water cannon threw him against the hatch. He also had a small but deep gash on one cheek. I brought out the first aid kit, and attended to his wounds. His nose wasn't broken badly, in that it wasn't deformed, but it started swelling immediately, and grew into the size of a tennis ball on his face. I cleaned his cut with hydrogen peroxide, and wrapped ice in a towel for him to hold against his nose, then refilled the ice tray and put it back in the freezer. Merwin didn't want to sit still for all of this treatment; he wanted to have another run at the tanker and whalers. He was one of the gentlest people I had ever met, until he got riled up over environmental issues. Then he became like a bulldog. No wonder he had gone to jail back in the 1970s.

"We have to go after them again!" His voice had changed because his nose was plugged with blood.

I shook my head. "If I thought we could change anything here, believe me, I would. But all we'll do is get killed. We'll be more effective in the future if we stay alive."

He dropped his head and nodded. He knew I was right. "Yeah, I guess so."

"Does it hurt a lot?"

He nodded again.

"I'll give you some painkillers, and you'll have to make yourself as comfortable as you can. Keep your nose higher than your heart, and hold ice against it to try and keep the swelling down."

"But what are we going to do now, Captain? We've got to stop the tanker from refuelling the *Nisshin Maru*."

"What's that?"

"The big whaling factory ship. The whalers bring their whales to her, and she cuts them up and prepares them for the market right on the ship. Without her, the whalers have to go back to Japan with only the whales they can carry, which is a lot fewer. We can't let the tanker refuel the *Nisshin Maru*, we just can't. Please tell me we're not returning to Tasmania." Merwin pleaded as though it were life and death. For the whales, it was.

"We're not going back yet. We're either going to follow those whalers south, or stay and watch the tanker. I'm not sure which."

Merwin smiled with relief behind the ice pack. "I knew you had it in you, Captain. And I know you'll make the right decision."

I wished I felt as confident as he did. I didn't see how we could make any difference here at all. But I wasn't ready to leave yet either.

Once the whalers finished refuelling—which took several hours—they headed out on the hunt again. It was light now. As I watched them turn around and face south, I had to fight down feelings of hatred towards them. They were on their way to kill whales. I wanted so much to stop them. Should we follow them, or stay with the tanker? What was the smartest thing to do? I looked at Merwin. He had fallen asleep again. His head was propped up on pillows, his nose completely plugged, and his snoring sounded like a clogged drain. I had to decide. The tanker hadn't refuelled the *Nisshin Maru* yet, and if she didn't refuel, she would have to return to Japan without more whales, and the smaller ships would have to return, too.

I decided to stay with the tanker, just hoping we might find a way to keep it from refuelling the *Nisshin Maru*. Besides, the whalers were smaller and faster, and we probably couldn't keep up with them.

All of the time that Merwin slept, the tanker slowly sailed

slightly south of west, getting closer to the Southern Ocean all the time, and perhaps she had crossed the 60th parallel already, I wasn't sure. We stayed half a mile away, on the surface, and I spent a lot of time watching her through the binoculars for any sign of activity. There was none. Then, after five hours or so, we had visitors. Welcome ones. Through the open portal I heard a blast of air. Our whales had returned.

It amazed me they could find us so easily. It amazed me even more they would want to. They must have become fond of us, too, mother and calf. It was too bad Merwin was sleeping, because it would have picked up his spirits to see them. But I really didn't want to wake him. He would need rest to recover from his wounds. In his absence, I did my best to sing to the whales. I put on the harness, climbed onto the hull, and sang "Frères Jacques" until I couldn't stand hearing it anymore. Then I tried "Scarborough Fair," and a few other songs that I knew. At first, I felt silly, and was afraid I'd just scare them away. But when I saw the mother whale look more closely at me, I realized she was really listening. I could tell. She seemed to like "Scarborough Fair" the most. There was a sparkle in her eye when I sang it, and she slapped her tail, so I sang it over and over again. I wondered if she realized there were ships down here that wanted to kill her and her baby. I think she did. Yet she never swam away. I wondered why she never did.

Everything that happened after that happened as if in a dream, where nothing anyone did could have stopped it or made any difference. It sure felt that way, perhaps because it was so violent, and perhaps because it happened so fast.

I heard a beep on the radar—a single vessel in the water, coming north towards us—and I knew in my heart that it was the *Nisshin Maru* even before I could see her through the binoculars. I spotted her at five miles because she was so big, and sat high in the water. I went back inside and looked at Merwin. He was still sleeping. His face was black and blue; he was exhausted. He might not forgive me later, but I decided not to wake him.

I went back outside and watched as the hulking factory ship approached. There was nothing I could do to prevent her from refuelling. She was as long as the tanker but sat higher in the water. There was blood on her bow. I didn't realize she did more than slaughter the whales that other ships caught for her. She caught them, too. Had I known that, I would have sailed away as fast as possible, and led the mother and calf away. But it didn't occur to me. Now, it was too late.

The sailors on the *Nisshin Maru* saw the mother whale snorting, and decided to catch her before refuelling. It didn't take them long. Their weapon was a powerful gun that shot an exploding harpoon. The harpoon was tied to a rope. Once a whale was shot with the harpoon, there was no escape. By the time I realized what they were doing, and tried to put the sub in their way, they had turned around and positioned themselves for a strike. Their ship was amazingly agile for her size, nothing like the tanker. To my horror I heard a loud bang, and right before my eyes the harpoon shot out from the bow of the ship, and I heard it strike and explode inside the head of the mother. She attempted to dive, but couldn't. She was dying. I heard her cry, and my heart broke. A wave of pain flooded through me, and suddenly I knew that what Sheba had foretold, had come to be.

Desperately, the mother whale turned towards me, and I saw her enormous eye, and the pain in it, and the worry that she had for her baby. How I wanted to tell her that it would be okay; that I would protect her baby. But I knew I couldn't promise it. I could only promise that I would try.

I felt such anguish in my heart. Every muscle in my body was tight. Every molecule inside of me knew I had to protect the baby whale, and I begged that the whalers would pass her by because she was so young. But they didn't.

"No!" I screamed, and tried again to put the sub between the ship and the whale, but the baby would not leave her mother, and the sailors on the *Nisshin Maru* could easily spot and target her. As they readied for a second strike, I grabbed the flare gun, aimed it as well as I could, and shot it. "Bang!" went the gun, and then "Bang!" went the harpoon once more. But the flare struck the bow just below the harpoon gun, and the harpoon shot out high, with its rope snaking after it, and missed the baby whale by ten feet. I didn't wait for them to reload; I shot the flare gun again. This time the flare went over the railing and onto the deck. I heard another bang, but this time I think it was the fire of a rifle. I ducked my head below the hatch. Were they firing at me, or just trying to warn me? I couldn't tell. I fired one more flare, then jumped inside and motored closer to the baby. I heard pinging on the hull, and knew now that they were firing rifles at the sub. I was not afraid of that, their bullets could not hurt the sub, but I was afraid they might shoot the harpoon at us. If it hit, and the tip exploded, it might puncture the hull, and prevent us from diving. If it hit us below water level, we would sink.

We had to get out of here, now. I could only hope that the baby whale would follow us. I hit the dive switch, and we began to descend. In the last few seconds before the hatch shut, I poked my head out and shot four flares at the harpoon gun in rapid succession. I didn't wait to see if any of them were on target. I just hoped they were.

Chapter Twenty-seven

MERWIN WOKE A SHORT while later, raised his head without opening his eyes, and asked what was happening. I thought he was still asleep. Nothing, I said. Go back to sleep. So he did. He was exhausted by his injuries, and the work of being at sea. I surfaced a couple of hundred feet from the *Nisshin Maru*, and went back outside.

The factory ship was positioning herself next to the tanker. The mother whale was pulled onto the stern of the ship by her tail. The beautiful life in her, her sweet personality and sweet songs were gone. She was a lifeless carcass now. Her blood had turned the water red. The *Nisshin Maru* had done what it was designed to do, and was now preparing to refuel.

I didn't see the baby whale on the ramp, and so had to assume it had escaped.

As I leaned against the hatch with my head on my arms, I wished I could have traded Sheba's prophesy for another wound to my arm, instead of the death of the mother whale. It all seemed so hopeless to me now—the struggle to save the planet—when there were so very many people who just didn't care, who were so destructive, and willing to do anything to make a dollar. I understood now that what Margaret had said was probably true, that it was too late to save the Earth. It wasn't because we didn't have the technology to do it—we did. It was because we were so destructive. Now I knew who the enemy was: it was us. As I watched the mother whale being dragged up the ramp, I felt a cloud of despair come down over my eyes, and a searing pain settle in my heart.

Only then did I hear the radar. It had been beeping all this time, but I had been too upset to hear it. I rushed inside to look. Two vessels were just three miles away, and were coming fast. I hurried outside again with the binoculars, and scanned the horizon. It was the *Steve Irwin* and *Bob Barker*.

I motored closer, and watched as the crew of the *Nisshin Maru* tried frantically to gather the hoses from the tanker and begin fuelling. But the sea was not cooperating. The swells were growing bigger every hour. The sky had darkened. The wind was strong now. I could tell by how frantic their movements were that they needed the oil desperately. The last thing they wanted to see was the Sea Shepherd Society.

The Shepherd ships came onto the scene like two wild hounds. They circled the two larger ships with an agility and closeness that astonished me. They were clearly not afraid of colliding with the *Nisshin Maru*, but were more careful around the tanker. The *Bob Barker* took a position in front of the bow of the giant whaler, while the *Steve Irwin* boldly proceeded to sail between the two ships. I saw Captain Watson on the bow, holding a bullhorn. He looked furious. I motored as close as I dared, and heard him issue a dire warning.

"You are in direct violation of the Antarctic Treaty! You are forbidden below the 60th parallel. Sail north now! We will escort you out of these waters."

Captain Watson repeated the message over and over, as the *Steven Irwin* squeezed between the sterns of the tanker and factory ship. But sailors from the *Nisshin Maru* began shooting water cannon onto the *Steve Irwin*, which she shot back. And then, unbelievably, the whaling ship steered into the environmentalist ship, and rammed her up against the tanker. I heard the terrible grinding together of hundreds of feet of steel, like gigantic steel monsters battling. The ships tossed and pitched wildly in the swells. The *Nisshin Maru* pulled away, and rammed again, and the blow turned the *Steve Irwin* sideways, which it then took advantage of by ploughing into the stern of the *Nisshin Maru*. It struck with such force, the whole whaling ship shook sideways in the water. And all of this time, water cannon shot back and forth between the two decks.

The battle raged on for over an hour, causing damage to all four ships. Captain Watson stayed on the bullhorn, informing the whaler and tanker that they were breaking international law. Not only was the tanker forbidden below the 60th parallel, the *Nisshin Maru* was also, because her bow was not reinforced to deal with Antarctic ice, which was required by international law. "You're breaking the law! Go back to Japan!" Captain Watson thundered. His voice was severe and threatening. After over an hour of extremely violent clashing between the ships, one thing became absolutely clear: the *Nisshin Maru* was not going to get any oil. And she must have needed it badly because she suddenly broke out of the fight, pointed her nose north, and cranked up her engines. Black smoke billowed out of her stern. She was damaged. She was limping home with her tail between her legs. Captain Watson declared over the bullhorn that the *Bob Barker* would escort her. The *Steve Irwin* would escort the tanker back above the 60th parallel.

I followed them. I would have liked to follow the *Nisshin Maru*, but even as damaged as she was, she was too fast for us. So we trailed behind the tanker, and her fierce escort. Within just a few hours we crossed back over the 60th parallel. As I caught up to the two ships, I heard Captain Watson give one final warning over the bullhorn: "*Don't come back!*" Then the *Steve Irwin* turned, and headed south once more. She still had the smaller whalers to chase. As the ship passed us, I stood up in the portal and gestured with my arm that I would follow the tanker back to Australia. Captain Watson waved to me, and I waved back. I didn't think I ever felt so proud as I did at that moment. But my pride was overshadowed by the sorrow I felt inside, and I was glad that from the distance no one could see the tears streaming down my face. The Sea Shepherd Society had saved hundreds of whales by preventing the whaling ships from refuelling, but it was a cruel enemy we were fighting, and I felt hopeless for it. Margaret's words weighed so heavily in my mind.

A few hours later, Merwin stirred in the bow. Hollie's tail was wagging, and he was sticking his nose close to Merwin's face, very gently sniffing at his wounds. He could smell blood. Hollie was an extremely sympathetic dog, and would stay with you when you were sick or injured. I put on a pot of tea, and a pot of porridge. The fresh milk was gone; we would have powdered milk. I peeled the last of the oranges and bananas. I wanted to keep busy. Merwin would want to know all that had happened, and I wasn't sure what to tell him. One part of me felt I should simply tell him everything exactly as it had happened. That's what I would have wanted if I were in his shoes, and I felt he deserved that. But another part of me wondered if that would be a mistake. I would tell him about the battle between the ships, for sure, and the outcome, and why we were following the tanker back to Australia. But did I need to cause him sorrow by explaining that the whale he loved so much had been slaughtered? What would that accomplish? That's what troubled me: I didn't want to cause him the pain that I was feeling. It was too discouraging.

"Good morning, Captain."

I took a peek at the clock. It was late afternoon. "Good afternoon."

"I hear the engine running full force. Where are we sailing?"

"North. We're following the tanker back to Australia."

"She's going back? That's great!"

"Yes, it is."

"How did it happen? Did I miss anything?"

"Yah, you missed a few things. There was a skirmish between the Sea Shepherd Society and the big whaling ship and tanker."

"The *Nisshin Maru*? You saw her? And you didn't wake me? Why didn't you wake me? I could have helped."

Merwin's nose was still swollen like a ball. His face was black and blue.

"Sorry. I figured you needed the rest."

He got to his feet, but was dizzy and unsteady. I had definitely made the right decision.

"I can't believe I missed all the action. What did the big whaling ship look like?"

"Bloody, and ugly."

"And where is she now?"

"On her way back to Japan."

"Really? That's fantastic! Gee, I can't believe I slept through that."

"You must have needed it. I'm making porridge. The tea is ready."

Merwin picked up a cup and poured himself some tea. He saw the powdered milk. "The fresh milk is all gone?"

I nodded. "It's time to go home." I meant him. I wasn't going home.

He sighed. "Ahhh . . . I suppose so. I wish I could have seen everything that happened, but at least the whales are safe now. Did you see our whales again?"

I nodded again, but avoided his eyes. "Yes, I saw them for a little while. Then they swam away." I felt terrible lying to him. I wished we were on land right now. Hollie and I would go for a long walk, like a couple-of-weeks long.

"Whew! That's good. Those whales are very special. I really love them. I swam with them, you know. You've got pictures, right?"

"Right."

"Thank Heavens they escaped the whalers."

"Yah."

"Do you see now why Captain Watson is my hero?"

"Yes, I do."

He was mine, too.

Chapter Twenty-eight

THE FIGHT BETWEEN THE Sea Shepherd Society and *Nishin Maru* had been filmed by both sides, and clips from the films found their way onto Australian TV. Unfortunately, they included footage of me in the portal of the sub, removing doubt in anyone's mind that I was the one who had sabotaged the tanker in Perth. How could I talk my way out of it now when I was caught on camera trying to do it again? We only learned this because Merwin was listening to the radio on our way back. That made us think that the tanker we were following had probably called the authorities to say that she was being followed by a submarine. We had to sail away from her. While many people might celebrate the actions of the *Steve Irwin* and *Bob Barker*, the news broadcaster had used the words "troublemaker" to describe us. And if we got caught now, Merwin would be in just as much trouble as I would.

In an effort to try to reduce the risk, we came up with a plan to get Merwin to shore without entering the three-mile zone. The navy and coast guard would almost surely chase us within the two-hundred-mile economic zone now, and definitely within the twelve-mile territorial zone. If they caught us, they would arrest us, tow the sub to shore, and we'd go to jail to await trial. And who knew how long that would take?

That was dangerous enough, but entering the three-mile zone, especially submerged, would likely be considered an act of terrorism at this point, and they'd probably shoot first, and ask questions later. We'd have to be insane to do it. Also, the closer we came to shore, the harder it would be to escape if we were spotted.

Our plan was to wait for good weather conditions, and then Merwin would paddle the inflatable kayak in from about three and a half miles offshore. He would leave with enough time to land before twilight, climb a cliff, and light two fires in the dark, side by side, so that I could see them from offshore. That would be his signal that all was well, and I would sail away.

If I never saw the fires, I would motor in at periscope depth, and search for him. I'd be able to see him through the periscope for most of the way while it was still light, and wouldn't leave until I saw the fire signal. I wondered if it would be too far for Merwin to paddle in his condition, but he insisted he was fine, and would enjoy the exercise. He assured me that paddling a kayak was something he could do well. After seeing him in the cold water with the whales, I had to admit he was tougher than I had thought.

We wanted to choose a spot that was isolated, yet not too far from a road. It would be dark soon after he landed, but he'd have his sleeping bag, and could catch some sleep before a long day's walk back to society. I felt badly for all the trouble he'd have to go through, but he convinced me he was looking forward to the adventure. I could relate to that, too. Hollie and I would have traded places with him in a heartbeat.

After poring over the map, we chose the coastline outside of Port Arthur, next to Tasman National Park. It was too far from Hobart for Merwin to walk, but there was a road there, and he said he would be able to hitchhike. Tasmania was a hitchhiker's paradise, he said, because people were so friendly, and hitchhiking was a respected way to get around. He picked up hitchhikers all the time. That was something I could believe. .

We slipped away from the tanker a little over two hundred miles from Tasmania. She veered very slightly to portside, suggesting she was heading west of Tasmania, and likely towards Melbourne. We veered starboard. From the air, she'd be easy enough to spot, and so would we, by anyone who knew to look for us in her wake. On our own, we'd be almost impossible to find in the vast open sea.

While we were following the tanker, we had to continue taking turns keeping watch and sleeping, but once we sailed away from her, we were able to stop, submerge, shut everything off, and sleep. There was no chance the tanker would turn around and head back to the Southern Ocean now; she had come too far.

Merwin was in great spirits. He had the adventure he had wanted. He had learned how to sail a submarine, and had swum with whales. That he had been beaten up by a water cannon didn't seem to bother him at all. I was glad I had decided not to tell him about the slaughter of the whale, and the longer we sailed, the more I felt that that was the right decision. It would have ruined his happy memories, and he probably wouldn't have recovered as quickly from his wounds. He wondered why I was so moody, and said several times he felt I was holding something back. I denied it, and just shrugged. What could I say?

We reached the area offshore from Tasman National Park, and spent twenty-four nerve-wracking hours waiting for the sea to calm. But it never did. Staying outside of the three-mile zone proved to be a lot more difficult that I had expected because there were so many peninsulas, bays and islands. You could be ten miles from the main coast, yet only two miles from a small peninsula jutting out into the sea. With the strong swells came a strong current, continually pushing us closer to shore. Merwin said that I shouldn't worry, and was keen to get into the kayak and have a paddle. But the swells were almost ten feet high, and I'd lose sight of him in less than quarter of a mile. No problem, he said, he was an experienced kayaker, and I should trust that he knew what he was doing. I didn't feel so confident. Merwin seemed to have a little of what Margaret had in abundance—the sense of being ready to die when your time was up. I shared no such feeling.

And so, as twilight was approaching on the second day, I motored in to just a mile offshore from Crescent Bay, not far from Port Arthur, and told Merwin to get ready. We would surface just long enough to inflate the kayak—ten minutes or so—he would jump in, and paddle straight to shore. Once he was in the kayak, I would submerge and motor back outside of the three-mile zone, keeping an eye on him as well as I could through the periscope. When he reached the beach, he'd climb the cliff and light the fires.

In my last command to him, I told him to wear the wet suit for the paddle in. He emphatically insisted that it wasn't necessary. I emphatically insisted that it was. What if he fell out of the kayak?

"I won't," he said.

As much as I liked Merwin, I was glad that I wouldn't be his captain much longer. Every order I gave was met with an argument. He was lucky he wasn't sailing with pirates, because they probably would have made him walk the plank for insubordination.

"How do you know? You fell off the sub."

"True, but . . ."

"Anyway, it's an order. We shouldn't waste time arguing over it. It's getting dark."

He turned his face into a pout. With his nose all red and swollen he looked a bit like a circus clown who had gotten into a fight, and lost.

We raised the portal above the surface just a couple of feet, threw the wet suit out on a rope, and gave it a good soak. Then we pulled it in and submerged again. I helped Merwin get into the suit. He complained the whole time.

"Now I'm taking two important things from you, Captain: your kayak, and your wet suit. Here! You have to take this." He reached over and slapped his cap on my head. It felt hot and sweaty, but I couldn't take it off without insulting him. "I was supposed to buy you a new wet suit."

"I can get another one along the way, and I have the rubber dinghy. I don't need a kayak, too. Thanks for the hat." I never mentioned that the kayak had been a gift from Ziegfried and Sheba before I left Newfoundland. I didn't have to wonder if they would agree with me giving it to Merwin in this situation; I knew they would.

"Well, I'll just keep them for you anyway, until the next time you visit . . . after all of this nonsense is over and your name is cleared."

He sounded so confident that that would happen. I hoped he was right.

Once Merwin was suited up, I surfaced again, opened the hatch, inflated the kayak, and tied it to a rope that I tied to a handle on the portal. I helped Merwin up the ladder, down onto the hull, and into the kayak, then carried up his sleeping bag and knapsack. The waves were lifting us up and down like a merry-go-round, but at least they weren't cresting, and so wouldn't spill into the kayak. There were no lights on the beach or cliff, but the moon was out, and he could keep his direction with that. I expected him to take no more than half an hour to reach the beach, fifteen minutes to climb the cliff, and another fifteen to collect wood and start a fire. If I didn't see the fire signal in an hour and fifteen minutes, I'd turn around and come looking for him.

"Wait two hours, Captain." He was sitting in position and ready to go.

I shook my head. "If I don't see the fires for two hours, I'll assume you're dead."

"You're too cautious, Captain." He smiled as he untied the rope.

"You're not cautious enough."

"Was it a good trade ... *Alfred*? Did you learn enough about environmentalism from me?"

I nodded. "Yes, I did. Was it a fair trade for you?"

He pushed himself off with the paddle. "More than fair. What was the best thing you learned?"

I tried to think quickly; there were so many things. My mind went back to the anthill. "Uhh ... every effort matters."

"That's good. I like that."

"What was the best thing you learned?"

His answer surprised me. "I'm a sculptor, not a naval engineer. Goodbye, Captain!" He paddled a few times, and quickly disappeared over the top of a wave.

I looked up at the moon. A cloud was covering it now, but you could still see enough light to navigate by it. I watched as Merwin appeared on the tops of a few more waves. He was moving quickly away from the sub. I felt confident he'd reach the beach without trouble. I shut the hatch, climbed down inside, submerged to periscope depth, and motored outside of the three-mile zone.

Almost an hour exactly from when he pushed off, I spotted a faint light in the dark. A few moments later, I saw another one beside it. I felt a burst of joy inside. Merwin was a wonderful person. I would miss him.

But as I stared at the two signal fires, I couldn't help thinking of the two whales we had befriended: the mother who had followed us, who had inspired us, and enjoyed our singing, and then died so horribly at the hands of the whalers; and her baby . . . and my joy slipped into sadness. I wondered where her calf was now. Was it old enough to fend for itself? Would it seek the company of other whales? Would it escape the whalers? I could only hope so.

Who were these whalers anyway? Weren't they just people like anybody else, with families, and homes, and dogs and cats for pets? Didn't their children go to school, and didn't they read them stories before bed at night? Suddenly I realized that it wasn't enough for me to learn how to save the planet. I needed to understand how people could be so destructive in the first place. Why, when whales were probably the nicest creatures on Earth, would anyone kill them so mercilessly? More than anything else, that's what I needed to know. And to find out, I knew I had to go to where the killers of whales lived—Japan—and see them for myself.

Chapter Twenty-nine

"IT'S TIME TO SERVICE the sub, Al. She needs new paint. You're probably carrying barnacles all over the world. That's not very efficient. I want to clean out the motor, flush all the systems, check the hull for cracks, check the propeller for cracks. It's time to come home."

"I know."

I was calling Ziegfried from a phone booth outside a small general store that sold fishing tackle and surfboards. I had moored the sub in the shelter of an alcove beneath Green Cape lighthouse, on the mainland of Australia. Although it was risky coming ashore, we really didn't have any choice; we would starve if we didn't.

"She wasn't made for beating up whaling ships."

"I know."

"So you're coming then?"

"Uhh . . . yes, definitely . . . eventually."

I heard Ziegfried sigh on the other end of the phone. It was morning in Australia—afternoon of the day before in Newfoundland. "Where are you headed, Al?"

"Japan."

"Japan?"

"Just for a little while. Then I'll come home."

There was a long pause. "Gee, I've always wanted to visit Japan. Maybe I should come and meet you there."

"*Really?* Would you come?" I felt a shiver of excitement.

"I don't know. I'll have to think about it, and talk it over with Sheba. She's standing beside me, waiting to talk to you. Take care of yourself, Al. You sound beaten up. Stop chasing ships that are bigger than yourself."

"Okay." But they were *all* bigger than me. "I really hope you will come to Japan."

"I'll give it serious thought. I miss you, buddy."

"I miss you, too."

"Here's Sheba."

There was a longer pause as Ziegfried handed the phone over. I could imagine him quickly explaining things to her. Then I heard Sheba speaking. The softness of her voice made me think of warm wind blowing over hot sand.

"My dear boy, you are all right?"

"Yes, I'm fine."

She paused. "No, you're not, you're wounded. I can hear it in your voice, and I can feel it in my heart."

"I'm fine, really."

"It happened, then?"

"Yah, it did."

"It was your heart that was wounded."

"Yes."

She sighed. "Life is a journey, Alfred, both joyful and painful. It seems we cannot have one without the other."

"I guess so."

"A letter came for you."

"A letter . . . ? Really? Who is it from?"

"It's postmarked from India."

"It must be from Melissa and Radji."

"I don't think so. It just says, 'Margaret.' But there's an address. Do you want me to open it and read it to you?"

"Yes, please." Wow, a letter from Margaret. How strange. I couldn't wait to hear it.

"She has nice, old-fashioned handwriting. She must be a nice lady, is she?"

"Yah, sort of. But I don't know how she sent me a letter. The last time I saw her she was in the middle of a storm at sea."

"Well, let me read it."

"Okay."

My Dear Alfred,

I found this address inside the cover of the book you lent me, and thought I would write you a letter in the hope it will reach you. I know that if it is meant to, it will. By now you must be in Australia. You might be interested to know that as soon as I started reading the Bhagavad Gita, *I became so inspired to visit India, that I started up the engine of my boat, and ran it through the storm, and didn't stop until I reached Kanyakumari, the most southern tip of India. There, I sold it to a man who has never sailed before. And so, my boat's journey continues without me.*

Brutus and Clive have retired from sea also. They have shaved, changed clothes, and taken positions in a tattoo and jewellery shop in Kanyakumari. You wouldn't recognize them. They look very Indian now. I bought a train ticket north, followed my instincts, and am now working on an organic farm that is inspired by a New Zealander with a wondrous philosophy. They have even made a film of him. It is called One Man, One Cow, One Planet. *Please do look for it. Whoever would have dreamed we might save the planet with cow dung? I want to thank you, my young friend, for rescuing me from my doldrums and giving me a new lease on life. Should you ever find the time to write me a letter, I would dearly love to hear from you. My address is on this envelope. You have inspired me, my courageous young submariner. In turn, I hope the writings of Thoreau are finding a home in you.*

With great affection, Margaret.

After I said goodbye to Sheba and Ziegfried, and stepped out of the phone booth, I felt my heart lift like a bird in the wind. I had gotten so used to Margaret's pessimistic view that I thought it was cut in stone. I didn't know why, but I had been using it as a sort of gauge with which to measure everything. There were things about us that were similar. We were both very stubborn, both sailing the world on a small vessel, both unafraid of storms and whatever might come our way. It almost felt as if she were an older version of me. Now, she had thrown away her pessimism like an old shoe, and given herself a brand new beginning. I found that so inspiring. Perhaps things were not so hopeless after all.

When I left the phone booth, I opened the door to the store, and stepped inside. In my excitement, I had forgotten to hide Hollie in the tool bag. He walked in beside me and looked all around like it was nobody's business. Like me, he was hoping there was something good to eat. Behind the counter sat a large, muscular man with tattoos on his neck and arms. He had a stern looking face, but was friendly enough. I was wearing Merwin's sandy-coloured hat, with the faded golden dragon on the front, and my month-old beard, with a tint of red. I had been told that my mother's hair had red in it.

"G'day!"

"G'day."

"First time here?"

I nodded. He looked down at Hollie, then back at me. "You don't look like a surfer or a fisherman, you must be a sailor or hitchhiker. Which is it?"

"Sailor. Do you have any potatoes?"

"At the back of that aisle. You must be sailing with your family. Did they send you in for potatoes?"

"They said I should pick some up if I happened to see any." I hated lying, but didn't know what else to say. I carried three bags of potatoes up to the counter. "What about beans?"

"First shelf. On the bottom. Where did you moor your boat?"

"Below the lighthouse."

"Below the *lighthouse*?" He sounded startled. I should have given a different answer. "Why didn't you moor in the harbour, at Eden?"

"Ahh . . . I don't know. We saw the beach, and everyone wanted to walk there." That much, at least, was true. I gathered ten cans of beans in my arms and carried them up to the counter.

"It's pretty rough below the lighthouse. You must have a heavy-duty anchor."

"Yah." I found the peanut butter and jam, and carried five jars of each up to the counter.

"Somebody loves peanut butter and jam." He stared into my face. "The whole crew?"

"Yah." That was true, too.

"How big is your boat?"

"Twenty-five feet."

"Catamaran?"

"No, just a regular sailboat."

"Wood, or fibreglass?" Now he was starting to sound suspicious.

"Wood." That was partly true. "Do you have any bread?"

"Third row, top shelf."

I brought four loaves up. I could freeze two. I went looking for cookies and candy. We had to get out of the store before he got any more suspicious. "You don't have any other vegetables by any chance, do you?"

"There are carrots in the fridge. Looks like your family is making you do all the work. It's a long hike to the lighthouse. Are you on foot?"

"Yah." I carried the carrots and cookies up to the counter. The candy was on the wall behind him. He turned around when he saw me staring at it.

"Let me guess: everybody on your boat loves candy?"

I nodded. "Yah." That was true, too.

He looked more closely at me, then down at Hollie. He was about to say something, but stopped. "Which ones?"

"The peppermints and toffees, please."

"How many bags each?"

"Ten."

He pulled them off the wall and started adding up the bill. I stared at the pile on the counter. I didn't know how I was going to carry it all back to the sub. I'd have to make two trips. First I'd get it out of the store, then split it up, and hide half of it in the bushes. He seemed to be reading my mind.

"I've got a little two-wheel trolley you can borrow." He

pointed to it. "You can carry all your groceries in it, and just leave it at the lighthouse. I'll pick it up later, or my friend will bring it in."

"Really? Thank you. That would be a great help."

"No problem. Here." He pulled out the trolley and loaded it up. I stood by and watched. Then he finished adding the bill. "One hundred and fifty-seven dollars and twenty-three cents."

I dug out my money.

"That's an expensive bill for someone who just came in for potatoes."

I smiled awkwardly. "I didn't just come in for potatoes."

He nodded, gave me my change, and didn't say anything more. I started out the door. "Goodbye. Thank you."

He just nodded again. He was definitely suspicious now. I could feel it. At least he didn't follow us out. Maybe we were going to get away with it. I pulled the trolley out, and Hollie trotted beside me. As I closed the door, I saw the man watching us. I turned and walked away quickly, pulling the trolley behind me. I felt my spine tingle.

We went about quarter of a mile down the road, when I heard him yell. "Hey! Hey!"

Shoot! He was coming after us. What should I do? Should I run for it? But what about the groceries? We really needed them. Could I toss some of them into the bushes before he got here, and come back for them later? No. There was no time for that. Desperately, I grabbed a bag of potatoes, a jar of peanut butter, a loaf of bread, and started to run.

"Come on, Hollie! *Run*!"

"Wait! Don't run! Wait!"

I turned around. He had stopped running, so I stopped. To get away from him I would have had to drop everything and really sprint. But I had paid for it, and hated to leave with nothing.

"Wait," he said. His voice was not threatening. "I know who you are."

"What do you mean?"

"I know who you are. I want to give you your money back."

"You want to give me my money back? Why?"

He held the money in his hand, and reached it out to me. "Here. Take it. I don't want your money."

"But . . . what about the groceries?"

"They're yours."

"I don't understand."

He rolled up his shirtsleeves. "Look."

I looked. On his right arm was a tattoo of a whale. On his left arm was a tattoo that said, "Save the whales!"

"I'm your ally, mate. I'm a supporter of the Sea Shepherd Society. I saw you on television. You guys are doing what I wish I could do. The least I can do is help out in other ways. Here, take your money back. I don't want it."

I reached out my hand and took the money. "Thank you . . ." I wanted to say more, but couldn't. My throat swelled up. I was so tired, and hungry, and moved by his kindness.

But I had to get a grip on my emotions. It was embarrassing.

"It's okay, mate. Just know that there are those of us rooting for you. Keep up the good work."

I managed to clear my throat. "Thank you."

"You're all right." He reached over, slapped me on the shoulder, turned around, and started back. I watched him go. Then I went over and picked up the groceries. As I pulled the trolley towards the lighthouse, every step felt a step lighter.

Epilogue

THE SEA TOSSED US AROUND like an untethered buoy. I had a pot of stew on the stove, a cup of tea in my hand, and my book on my lap. Hollie was happily chewing the end of a rope, but the movement of the sub kept rolling it away from him, and he had to pull it back with his paw. Seaweed was in a deep sleep. His webbed feet secured him to his spot. It would take a pretty big wave to shake him loose. Margaret's letter reminded me of something Thoreau had written. I opened the book to the first chapter and searched for the words. I felt less alone when I read Thoreau's words because it felt as though he were sitting right across from me, saying the words out loud, slowly, solemnly, and maybe with a twinkle in his eye.

What everybody echoes or in silence passes by as true today may turn out to be falsehood tomorrow, mere smoke of opinion, which some had trusted for a cloud that would sprinkle fertilizing rain on their fields. What old people say you cannot do, you try and find that you can.

I didn't yet know why they called Thoreau the father of the environmental movement, but I sure felt armed with his words. It made me wonder if words were our best weapon. Even Captain Watson, as fierce as he was on the sea, was fighting the whalers in the courts, too, and on television, where the weapons were words. Maybe I could learn to do that, too. I thought of Margaret, working on an organic farm in India. She was learning something new all over again. I thought of the tattooed man who gave me the groceries for free because he believed so much in the Sea Shepherd Society. Everyone who cared was helping in his or her own way, and every action mattered, big or small. That was something I learned from Merwin. As I got up to stir the stew, and turned to look at my resting crew, I felt my worries fade away like shadows in the night, and a strong conviction take their place. I felt I could remember the whales now without tears, those noble, intelligent, and beautiful creatures. We were sailing to Japan to face their killers.

ABOUT THE AUTHOR

Philip Roy lives in St. Marys, Ontario, with his family, and their 17-year-old cat. Continuing to write adventurous and historical young adult novels focusing on social, environmental, and global concerns, Philip is also delighted to be embarking upon *Mouse Pet*, his third book in the "Happy the Pocket Mouse" series (illustrated by Andrea Torrey Balsara), due out in the fall of 2015, as well as the eighth volume of the "Submarine Out-law" series, set in Japan (Ronsdale Press). Along with writing, travelling, running, composing music, and crafting folk art out of recycled materials, Philip spends his time with his growing family. Visit Philip at www.philiproy.ca.

More Adventures with Alfred & His Submarine

PHILIP ROY

Submarine Outlaw
978-1-55380-058-3 PRINT
978-1-55380-145-0 E-BOOK

Journey to Atlantis
978-1-55380-076-7 PRINT
978-1-55380-074-3 E-BOOK

River Odyssey
978-1-55380-105-4 PRINT
978-1-55380-117-7 E-BOOK

Ghosts of the Pacific
978-1-55380-130-6 PRINT
978-1-55380-136-8 E-BOOK

Outlaw in India
978-1-55380-177-1 PRINT
978-1-55380-178-8 E-BOOK

Seas of South Africa
978-1-55380-247-1 PRINT
978-1-55380-248-8 E-BOOK